The Unseen

Thea Harrison

From New York Times *bestselling author Thea Harrison comes the first of two explosive new stories set in the Elder Races world…. Dragos and Pia are back by popular vote!*

THIS STORY ENDS IN A CLIFFHANGER

Saying goodbye to their old life in the Wyr demesne in New York may be hard, but Dragos and Pia are determined to create a new life in the Other land of Rhyacia.

At first, everything seems idyllic. Rhyacia is paradisiacal. Accompanied by old friends and new allies, the future looks safe and bright for Dragos, Pia, and baby Niall.

But strange things are happening beneath the picturesque façade. Items move unaccompanied, buildings collapse without justifiable cause, and even the most Powerful residents of Rhyacia can provide no logical explanation for the events transpiring. Whispered rumors point to something called *the unseen.*

As Dragos and Pia investigate, they uncover a greater mystery than they could have imagined, and they realize the startling truth…

They're not alone in Rhyacia. The land Dragos had thought was uninhabited hides many secrets, a shocking history that's not quite ready to be buried, and something more.

Something ancient, evil, and hungry. Something that wants to consume Dragos and take everything he holds dear.

Something that just may be powerful enough to overcome the dragon…

This is book 1 in a series of 2 connected novellas. The first book ends in a cliffhanger.

Chapter One

"WHAT EXACTLY DO you pack when you're leaving Earth for good?" Pia murmured.

She stared at the huge pile of clothes and personal items she had heaped on the king-sized bed she shared with her husband and mate, Dragos Cuelebre, in the house they had built.

When she and Dragos had made the decision to leave the Wyr demesne in New York and move to the Other land of Rhyacia, they had agreed to not pack any household items. Everything they had required to furnish their spacious house in upstate New York would remain intact and ready for any time they might choose to return.

But that didn't make the impending move simple or easy. Their decision had propelled Pia into an intense buying spree for new household items that they sent into the Other land in regular shipments. Despite Pia's original intention to focus solely on their new baby Niall, she had been unable to remain detached from the process. This was to be her new home, and she needed to feel comfortable in it. She couldn't just step back and let someone else create the whole thing for her.

Color schemes had to be decided upon. Bedding, curtains, carpets (all of which meant the number of rooms and room dimensions needed to be decided upon), kitchenware, bath linens, and more—and every decision had to take into account that while Other lands were rife with magic, they existed in different dimensions from Earth and modern technologies such as electricity and gas-run vehicles didn't work. Goodbye, KitchenAid stand-up mixer and Keurig coffee makers. Hello, manual hand mixers and French press coffee makers.

What items of furniture would they transport, and what could be made on site? Rhyacia was roughly the size of Greenland. Currently it was a vast stretch of undeveloped land that Dragos had discovered and protected long ago in case he might decide to do something with it someday.

His contingency planning had become a reality. Now, the community in Rhyacia was new and growing at an exponential rate, fueled by Wyr who were leaving New York in huge droves as they enthusiastically embraced the new challenge.

Very soon what had once been a vast tract of pristine, undeveloped land would become a nation, and Rhyacia would be self-supporting in every conceivable way, but that hadn't happened yet. While money was no object in designing their house (a fact that still felt foreign and exotic to Pia), intensive thought and effort had to go into planning every detail, since most of what they wanted and needed had to be shipped in. Massive cargo caravans transporting a wide variety of goods including shelf-stable and freeze-dried food, tents, eco-friendly prefab housing, and other building materials crossed over to the Other land daily.

In the meantime, Dragos had to follow through with his decision to abdicate as Lord of the Wyr in New York—a position he had held for hundreds of years. He had been intensely busy both with building plans for their new house and working with the sentinels in New York to facilitate a transfer of power to Rune, his former First sentinel, who would act as regent until Pia and Dragos's oldest son Liam decided if he wanted to take over.

Because Dragos was often in New York, many of the household decisions Pia needed him to weigh in on had been made via FaceTime and text. Finally, after two months of intense activity, it was time to pack clothes and toiletries. They would leave for Rhyacia in two days.

Pia regarded the containers of blush, eyeshadow, mascara and lipstick she held in her hands. She wasn't clear on how rough the living conditions would be in the new settlement. How likely was it that she would want to wear makeup any time soon?

But this move wasn't exactly like they were traveling to another neighborhood with a strip mall located a few blocks away where she could buy anything she needed. If she didn't take things now, she wouldn't have access to anything like it again very easily.

Her gaze traveled to the nearby French doors, propped open to let in a warm afternoon breeze. Eva had taken Pia's youngest son Niall outside to give her a break so she could get some serious packing done. While Niall was a helpless two-month-old baby in his human form, in his Wyr form he was hell on four hooves.... And he liked to stay in his Wyr form.

Eva had changed into her canine Wyr form as well. She chased Niall's tiny streamlined bronze form across the freshly mown lawn. When Niall spun and lowered his equine head to point his horn at Eva, Pia laughed under her breath. That little boy loved to stab things. Eva barked at him, and he tore off in a different direction. Eva lunged in pursuit, and they disappeared from Pia's line of sight.

She loved everything about the scene outside. Her disaster baby; her best friend. Every detail of the landscaping had been a choice she'd helped to make. When she had first met and mated with Dragos, she'd had to learn to love his penthouse in Cuelebre Tower— and she'd succeeded. She'd made a few changes, claimed the kitchen as her own, and lavished all her attention on decorating their first son Liam's nursery.

This place was different. She and Dragos had chosen everything about it together. She had helped to create this home from the ground up, and she loved every inch of it.

Man, she was going to miss that KitchenAid mixer. Her chest constricted and the peaceful outdoor scene disappeared as her eyes flooded with moisture.

Firm footsteps sounded as Dragos walked up behind her. One massive hand came down to cover both of hers, makeup and all. He said in her ear, "Remember, we agreed. No plastic."

"I know what we said, but… none at all?" she asked in dismay. She picked up a plastic container of antiperspirant. It was her favorite brand. She'd been using it for forever.

"None." His tone was final. "We're not going to create a trash or pollution problem in Rhyacia."

Tilting one shoulder up, she sighed. "I don't disagree."

The heat from his tall, muscular body warming her back and legs eased some of the ache she was feeling. He buried his face in her neck and inhaled. His lips moved against her sensitive skin as he murmured, "Besides, I like the way you smell."

Mmm, delicious. But she would not give into the temptation to go boneless against him. She still had too many items outstanding on her To-Do list. "Did you ever consider the reason why you might like the way I smell is because of my choice in toiletries?" She pulled out her container of mascara and brandished it in front of his eyes. "I'm so fair, I'm almost an albino. Where do you think my eyelashes come from?"

"I have seen you plenty of times without your makeup, and you're gorgeous." He ran his mouth along the line of her jaw. "Unless I miss my guess, you're not wearing makeup right now."

"What does that have to do with anything?" she demanded.

He paused, then said cautiously, "This is a female thing, isn't it?"

To Dragos, the female experience was a vast continent filled with baffling mysteries and countless pitfalls, but at the moment she felt too sad to smile. Resting her cheek against the side of his head, she said, "Yes, this is a female thing."

"Hm." He scooped up her makeup and antiperspirant. "I'll take these."

"What?" she exclaimed. "Why? We haven't left for Rhyacia yet."

"You'll see." When she spun on her heel to confront him, he raised one sleek black eyebrow. His brutally handsome features were relaxed in an expression of subtle amusement. "That's all for now. Carry on."

Her mouth fell open to argue more, but he had already wheeled away and strode out of their bedroom suite.

"I was going to take a shower with some of that," she muttered crankily. Then what he had said hit her. She shouted after him, "What do you mean I *smell?*"

His deep laughter floated up the stairs. A few moments later she heard the distant sound of the front door opening and closing.

"It's not like any of that was special anyway." She made a face at the empty doorway and whispered,

"Because I'm just a New York girl who likes to shop at Target."

Without the distraction of Dragos's intense, vital presence, the ache welled up again. There was no one to watch or question what she did next. Burying her face in her hands, she let the tears come.

AFTER THAT, TIME sped up and felt inexorable. Thoughts like, *this is the second to last time I'll be eating toast at this kitchen counter* or *that's the last episode of* The Bachelor *I'll be watching for a while* kept floating through her mind, and she felt close to tears more often than not.

Late in the afternoon the next day, she walked around the corner of the downstairs hallway to find Dragos leaning one shoulder against the doorway to his office. He was dressed simply in a black T-shirt that stretched across his powerful broad chest and faded jeans that had seen better days, one booted foot kicked over the other. His arms were folded, the massive muscles in forearms and biceps delineated under the deep bronze skin.

He looked grim, but when he spoke, his voice was gentle. "When are you going to tell me what's bothering you?"

She stopped in her tracks, feeling flat-footed. So much for thinking that she had kept her inner upheaval private. She opened and closed her mouth a couple of times before she could say, "I promise I will when I've figured out the right words to say."

His hard, sexy mouth tightened. He didn't like that—but then, he never liked anything that refused to give him whatever he wanted the moment he demanded it. "Tell me now. I don't care if you use the wrong words."

She gave him a wry look. "Only someone who hasn't heard the wrong words could say that." At the baffled frustration in his expression, she said more softly, by way of apology, "I thought I was doing a better job of hiding things."

His frustration melted into anger. "You're not supposed to hide anything from me," he growled. Moving away from the doorway, he advanced on her, clamping both hands on her shoulders.

"I wasn't *intentionally* hiding things from you," she said as she looked up into his narrowed gold gaze. Anger sparked. "I'm not deceitful with you, ever. Period."

The tension in his hands eased. "I know."

Okay then. That was better.

"I'm working things out in my head," she told him. "I get to do that, you know. I get to sort through my thoughts and feelings to figure out what I *should* say, what I *want* to say, and what is even true about what I'm feeling. And that means I need to understand what I'm feeling before I can talk about it."

He scrutinized her features, then said grimly, "That sounds like a lot of bullshit and prevarication to me."

"Does it?" She blinked, more taken aback than ever. "I don't mean it that way. Dragos, we've only been together for a few years, and in that time we've gone through a lot of change. A lot. This move is more change, and it's a whopper. We're not wrong for deciding to go to Rhyacia, and we shouldn't back out of the decision, but I also get to feel my feelings over it." She looked around and felt her face crumple. "I love this house. This is our home, the one we built together. It doesn't mean I won't love our new home that we're also building together. But I don't love the new one yet."

Understanding eased his expression. He pulled her into his arms. She rested her cheek against his chest and slid her arms around his waist. He murmured into her hair, "Are we moving too fast? Do you want to take a couple more weeks before we cross over? Or even another month or two?"

Relishing the hard muscle underneath the cotton of his shirt, she shook her head. "No, but thank you for suggesting it. I think I'll feel better when we're over there and having our adventure, instead of being here and constantly saying goodbye to everything. At this point, I think it's just time for us to go." Then, because she wanted to be scrupulous, she added carefully, "That may not be quite everything I want to say, but it's the essence of what I'm working on. Since a lot of this was my suggestion, I feel like I should be handling things better than I am. When I figure out anything else that I need to talk about, I'll tell you. Okay?"

"Fair enough." His arms tightened before he let her go and stood back. "Come here. I have something for you."

"You do?" Wiping her face, she followed him into his office, looking around. While Dragos had never been anything less than welcoming and she certainly stepped inside whenever she felt like it, this room was definitely his domain. His personality was stamped all over the elegant, masculine furnishings.

A carved box sat on his desk. Even as her curious gaze fell on it, he scooped it up with one hand and presented it to her.

She gave him a sidelong smile then focused her attention on the box itself. Designed in an art nouveau style, the craftmanship was beautiful. Peacocks and butterflies adorned the top and sides, inlaid with amethyst, blue calcite, labradorite, citrine, and other stones she was unfamiliar with. She held it closer to absorb the details of the intricate, delicate carving. "This is remarkable."

"It's a commissioned piece." A hint of satisfaction entered his deep voice. "Nobody else has anything like this. The designs were created specifically for you. Open it."

She did and found smaller carved pieces inside, each one a delight, the wood polished to a deep golden glow. A familiar scent escaped the box as she had opened it. Comprehension began to dawn.

Exclaiming in delight, she set down the bigger box to pick out one of the smaller pieces inside. It was round and cylindrical, with lapis lazuli inlaid in a swirling pattern like ocean waves. It was shaped remarkably like…

A tube of lipstick?

She pulled off the cap and experimentally tried to twist the base, then watched in disbelief as a fresh, unused piece of her favorite lipstick rose out of the thin golden wood tube.

"You didn't," she said.

"Didn't I?" Smiling, he watched her explore the contents.

Carefully closing the lipstick again and setting it aside, she opened a slender box with a carved orchid on the top, inlaid with mother-of-pearl. Inside was a fresh palette of her favorite eye shadow, accompanied with a small, exquisite wooden application wand tipped with what looked like a small piece of natural sponge.

And then another box, this one with a seashell engraved on top and inlaid with abalone. Inside, she found her favorite blush, with a brush made of wood and sable. In an oval cylinder, inlaid with rose quartz, she found her favorite antiperspirant gel had been injected into the container. There wasn't a piece of plastic in any of the toiletries in the box.

The thing about feeling your feelings: sometimes they were so huge and complex, you couldn't figure out how to put words to them.

Lifting her gaze, she met his. Her voice wobbled slightly as she said, "You had someone create these incredible works of art for me, and you made them put makeup from *Target* in them?"

Beginning to look baffled again, he shrugged. "They're your favorite, right?"

"Yes," she whispered, stroking the gorgeous lipstick case.

"I had the artisan create copies of every piece," he told her. "You can order more of anything, any time you're ready for it, and he'll ship a fresh box to you. When you've received it, you can send back the used one, and he'll clean it up and refill it with new cosmetics." One long finger hooked underneath her chin, and he tilted her face up. "Don't you like it?"

She said with perfect sincerity, "I think this is the nicest thing you've ever done for me."

He still looked faintly mystified as he stroked along her cheek with his thumb. "I've bought you plenty of jewelry that cost a hundred or a thousand times what this makeup box cost."

Amusement curved her lips. Yes, he had, and it was a measure of his love for her that he was able to actually *give* the jewelry to her after he had acquired it. But as much as she loved that the dragon gave her jewels, those outrageously expensive pieces never meant as much to her as they did to him.

This, however, was purely about her. He had seen her struggling to let go of something that was pretty minor in the grand scheme of life, and he had taken steps to make sure she didn't have to. He could have had the makeup inserted into disposable cardboard shapes, and that would have been astonishing and thoughtful enough, but, being Dragos, he had to turn the whole project into treasure.

"Thank you. I love it with all my heart," she said. Hooking an arm around his neck, she drew his head down to hers.

"That's all that matters, then," he said against her lips. His voice had turned husky.

She had told him what she could of the things she struggled with, but there were some things she could never tell him. Never. Savoring his mouth and every sensual detail of his long, hard body pressed against her, she locked down those secrets tight in the deepest, most private part of her soul.

After all, they had already discussed it, two months ago after Pia and Rune's mate Carling had been kidnapped. The kidnapping had been a ploy by a crazed and embittered Elf to trap and destroy Dragos Cuelebre, who was known throughout the Elder Races as the Great Beast. During that nightmare, Pia had been forced to give birth to Niall in a cave and had met Dragos's brother, Lord Azrael, the god of Death.

Once, she had just been a New York girl who wore makeup from Target and got freaked out over having feelings for a dragon. She was an herbivore who had to keep her Wyr nature secret, while he was the ultimate predator. Falling in love and mating with him had felt earthshaking and immense all on its own.

But coping long term with the reality of mating with Dragos was like opening an infinity of nesting puzzle boxes. As soon as she opened one and thought she had a grasp on things, she found another box to open, another reality even more immense than the one before.

She remembered the conversation they'd had after the kidnapping as if it had happened yesterday. *How many Primal Powers are there?* she had asked. *The Elder Races only have seven in their pantheon.*

You got me, Dragos had said with a shrug. *I don't really have anything to do with them, except I used to have a…let's call it a certain rapport with Azrael.*

He hadn't been lying, exactly; her truthsense was deeply attuned to him and she was certain of that. But his gold gaze had slid away from hers when he had said it.

And Azrael had said to her, *You, of all people, should know how closely related death and the dragon are.*

She did, or at least she had thought she had. But there were *consequences* to that close relation that she had never before queried, until then.

When she'd talked to Dragos, she'd tried to make light of it. To make it safe, as she'd asked him, *We're not going to talk about the pressures of godhood or anything like that?*

And he'd brushed the whole thing off. *Pia, what does godhood mean? Tiago is a thunderbird. More than half my sentinels have been worshipped as gods in Egypt. Look at the Djinn and what they can do. Hell, look at yourself in the mirror—look at yourself when you're in your Wyr form. Unless something or someone kills you, you are going to live indefinitely, and your blood heals any wound. That's pretty damn miraculous in my book. There are many of the Elder Races who have been called gods at one point or other in history, and just as many who have been called demons.*

His logic had been unassailable. He was right, but....

But.

Dragos was her husband, her mate, her dedicated lover, and most fierce protector, and yet in many ways he was still a total mystery to her. Some days, she couldn't help but run that conversation through her mind again. Some days, she felt just like a New York girl who had gotten lost on a lonely road in a country so foreign she didn't even know its name.

And the only thing that brought her home again was this: his mouth, his hands, his scent. Her body knew every exciting detail of his and craved it. She craved him.

When he shut the door to his office and turned back to her, his movements were tight with the hunger that drove him. She was already moving, stripping off her shirt and wriggling out of her jeans.

As she kicked out of them, he wound one hard arm underneath her hips and lifted her onto the desk. They often took their time with foreplay and teasing, laughing together under the velvet cloak of an indulgent midnight, but this was not one of those times.

He yanked off her underwear, and she eagerly wound her legs around his hips while she pulled his T-shirt over his head to reveal the heavy musculature of his tremendous chest. When he eased the thick, broad head of his erection against her opening, she was wet and ready. Her head fell back, eyes closed, as he entered her.

They fit together like the oldest, truest magic: yin and yang; female and male; dark and light.

It was only during times like these when she felt relief from the doubts and insecurities that plagued her. When all her doubts were vaporized in the heat of passion, and the deepest, most private part of her soul said to him, I don't care who or what you are. You're mine.

You're mine.

Chapter Two

FINALLY, EVERYTHING WAS done. Dragos had given away his demesne. It turned out, an old dragon could learn new tricks, do new things. Could decide on taking new adventures.

The gryphon Rune, Dragos's former First sentinel, and his Vampyre mate Carling left their home in Florida to settle in a spacious apartment in Cuelebre Tower that had been specially fitted with Vampyre safety shutters, and Dragos had to admit that was one thing he never thought he would see happen. Turns out, an old dragon could also let go of engrained habits. He had distrusted Carling for so long, it was only when Carling had been kidnapped with Pia that Dragos had finally been able to fully accept her relationship with Rune.

All necessary paperwork was completed, the t's were crossed, the i's dotted. The official shit had been vetted by demesne lawyers. As for the unofficial shit…

Well, the Wyr sentinels were well versed in handling any unofficial shit.

They'd had a huge going-away bash in the Tower ballroom. The food was fabulous, the liquor ever-flowing, and people gave them presents even though Dragos and Pia had specifically stated in the invitations, no presents, please. And if Dragos's eyes glazed over at the excruciating number of Wyr who got all fucking weepy at him, nobody mentioned it. Pia kept a close eye on him and rescued him whenever things became too heartfelt.

The main thing was, everybody survived and had a good time.

Pia got to dance with Quentin, her old friend and former employer. Now Quentin, a Wyr panther, was a sentinel—another thing Dragos had never thought to see—and he was mated to another sentinel, the harpy Aryal, who had the dubious honor of being the most insane female Dragos had ever met.

Aryal tried to needle Graydon, also a gryphon and one of Dragos's original sentinels, into a wrestling match. Graydon had resigned his sentinel position and was moving to Rhyacia with his mate, the Elven lady Beluviel. They were new parents also, and Pia and Beluviel were close friends. While Pia did have Eva, who was her best friend and personal bodyguard, Eva didn't have children, nor was she mated. It would be good for Pia to also have Beluviel in Rhyacia, and Dragos had to admit, it would be good for him to have Graydon.

Annoyed with Aryal's antics, Graydon kept brushing her off until she threw up her hands and walked away, only to circle around and tackle him from behind. That cleared a space around them quickly.

Startled into laughter, Beluviel dashed away from the pair. Graydon roared curses as he fought to get out of the harpy's clutches. A betting pool was established within moments; the inhabitants of Cuelebre Tower were well experienced with how to respond to this sort of thing.

As Quentin wandered away from the fight with Pia on his arm, Dragos heard him say to her with a smiling shrug, "She's my mate, not my problem."

Dragos and Pia's oldest son Liam took leave from college to attend the party, and Dragos used the opportunity to study Liam as his son cruised through the crowd, a smiling, easygoing predator.

Liam was one of the many changes Dragos and Pia had gone through. If Liam had grown like any other child, he would still be a toddler. Instead, being the progeny of two intensely magical and Powerful creatures, he had burgeoned into existence with the kind of speed reminiscent of the first generation of the Elder Races.

Now fully as tall and as powerfully built as Dragos, his handsome features, blond hair, and blue eyes were like catnip to most of the women and several of the men. He fended off advances with casual poise, and Dragos smiled to himself as he realized Liam had learned a lot more from college than schoolwork and magic spells.

He was the golden son, the heir apparent. New York was his for the taking if he wanted it, and New York was speaking its mind loud and clear as it said yes, please. But when the time came, would Liam choose to take over ruling the demesne in New York? There was no way to know yet how that story would play out.

Dragos kept the penthouse at the top of Cuelebre Tower. Maybe, eventually, he would give it to Liam, but that also had yet to be decided. For now, it remained his and Pia's.

He also kept most of the money. (There was quite a lot of it.) Sorting out the money was the biggest headache of everything, because Dragos had always treated his finances as fungible and moved funds from his personal and business accounts to the demesne, or back again as needed.

In the end, he kept his favorite business ventures, all of them steady money earners and capable of operating efficiently without his constant hand at the helm, and he resigned from the boards and signed over the stock from others. Nation building in Rhyacia was going to be expensive. He felt no compunction about keeping most of the liquid assets, while leaving the demesne enough in its operating budget to see it to the end of the first calendar year.

With the businesses he signed over and some decent management, the New York Wyr demesne would remain solvent and build back up to affluence within five to seven years. The rents alone from the businesses and restaurants located in Cuelebre Tower would fund the essential functions of the Wyr demesne. They had enough to pay the bills, all administrative, legal and sentinel salaries, and to keep the lights on. They would do just fine.

One night, when Dragos had traveled to New York for business and had left Pia and Niall at home upstate, the sentinels threw him and Graydon another unofficial bash at Quentin's bar. This one was a much more private and raucous affair. During it, Aryal and the others gave him a large, oddly shaped present. It stood waist-high, and when Dragos tore off the wrapping, he discovered it was a gold sundial.

"Get it?" Aryal nudged his shoulder. "It's a gold retirement watch! But this one will work in an Other land. Hahaha!"

As Dragos raised his eyebrows, Quentin said, "She's been waiting weeks to say that."

Aryal confessed. "Actually, it's so big it's gold plated—it's not solid. But it's plated with quality gold! We made sure of that when we stole it. Don't you fucking love it?"

A giant gold watch made with purloined treasure. Dragos laughed. "I do. I really fucking love it."

"Booyah," the gryphon Bayne said, eyes gleaming with a smile. "We thought you might."

Eventually, close to dawn, that party wound down too. Graydon walked away with a giant bag of cloth diapers and a case of antique scotch. Dragos returned to upstate New York with the sundial and a smile on his face.

All final tasks had been completed in a reasonable amount of time, and all challenges had been surmounted.

While Dragos would never lay claim to understanding women, he had listened to his wife air her issues and he had pleased her well with her gift of toiletries. For someone who knew he was not a very good man, he liked to think he was a good mate and husband. He was a good dragon.

Liam promised to visit them in Rhyacia within the next month. The sentinels swore they would rotate in visits for their vacations, and by the eagerness in their expressions, Dragos knew they meant it. Dragos, Pia, and Niall's clothes were packed. Earlier that day, Graydon and Bel, along with their baby daughter and Bel's cadre of dedicated Elven attendants, had already crossed over.

Everything was well in hand. Life moved on, even if not all of it was rosy. Over the weekend, Eva had broken the news that Elizabeth Creedy, one of Liam's old elementary school teachers, had died in a car crash on Friday night. That saddened Pia deeply as she had liked Miss Creedy, but Dragos barely remembered what the woman looked like.

"She was so young, only in her forties," Pia said. "And I don't think she had any family. I remember she once said the children in her classroom were her family. Liam's going to be sad to hear she died. She was so nice to him."

Liam had also grown at such an accelerated pace he hadn't stayed in one classroom for very long, so he hadn't formed lifelong attachments to anybody. Dragos was rather proud that he avoided mentioning that, since he knew he wasn't always the most tactful of creatures.

"Let's not interrupt him any further while he's at school," he suggested. "He's had enough disruptions this year. We can always break the news when he comes to visit."

Pia gave that some thought. "That makes sense, I guess."

The conversation moved on to other things, and the last hours of their remaining time on Earth flew by, until at last it was their final evening. Dragos looked forward to a good night of sleep and sex, not in that order, enjoying a great, homecooked breakfast in the morning, and making a leisurely crossing over to Rhyacia around midmorning.

Of course, that would be when things slid sideways, as they did every fucking time things went too fucking smoothly in his life.

THAT NIGHT, HE lounged on their bed watching the late-night news, feet crossed at the ankles. He was going to miss the twenty-four-hour news channels. He'd hired someone to compile a summary report each week of the world news, both human and Elder Races, and to collect various newspapers to have couriered to him. He might be withdrawing from Earth, but he wasn't going to stick his head in the sand. It always paid to stay informed.

Pia lay back against a pile of pillows. She had just finished nursing the baby, and Niall had fallen asleep on her chest. The French doors were propped open, as they so often were, to the cool evening air that smelled damp with impending rain.

Stroking the baby's dark, downy head, Pia crooned, "Who's my stabby little psychopath?"

Dragos chuckled as he curled a hand around her knee. "You better not let him hear you say it like that when he's in his Wyr form. He might get the idea that being a stabby little psychopath is a good thing."

"I would never." She grinned. "At the moment, he's just a baby and he doesn't know any better, but in his Wyr form he understands every single thing we say."

"Only goes to prove what I've been saying for centuries," he remarked lazily. "Animals are the most intelligent of all creatures."

"Yes, and that's not just the Wyr," she agreed. "Mundane animals are super smart too. Anybody who is a pet owner can vouch for that..." She frowned. "Mundane. Pet owners. Oh no." Holding Niall firmly, she lunged upright. "Dragos, get dressed. We need to go to Miss Creedy's house—we have to find out where she lived."

She spoke quietly so she didn't wake the baby, but the urgency in her words had him launching into action. *Eva,* he said telepathically as he yanked on a pair of jeans. *We need you now.*

Be right there, Eva replied. Even though he had probably woken her up, she sounded completely alert. *What's wrong?*

I don't know yet. He could already hear Eva running through the house toward them, so he switched to verbal speech. "What's going on, Pia?"

She had already eased Niall onto the bed and was dressing quickly too. "Miss Creedy rescued a dog while Liam was in her class. He adored that dog. Said it was the ugliest thing, but so sweet and smart, and it really loved to learn tricks." She looked at him, distressed. "She didn't have any family. What if nobody's thought about the dog and it's still at her house? It's been three days since she died."

"I'll find out her address." As former lord of the Wyr demesne, Dragos still had access to certain databases. He passed Eva in the hallway and jogged down the steps to his office.

"Eva—oh good, there you are," Pia said. "We need you to watch Niall for a while."

While Eva and Pia's voices floated downstairs, he logged into his computer and ran a few quick searches. When Pia's quick footsteps sounded in the doorway, he had already stood. He angled his way around the desk.

"Got it," he told her. "She lived on the other side of town. I can shapeshift and fly us there in a few minutes."

"Okay. Hold on." She dashed to the kitchen and came back carrying a Tupperware container filled with the bacon she had cooked for breakfast. "I hope somebody already thought to check her house for pets. If they haven't yet…well, I hope it's still alive."

Dragos didn't understand the need to keep pets. To

him, animals were either predator or prey—and since he was the ultimate apex predator, he didn't concern himself too much with the niceties of those distinctions.

But he did understand the emotions people attached to their pets, and he understood all too well the emotional upset that now darkened Pia's scent. And the thought of any mundane animal being neglected or abused was distasteful, to say the least.

"It's going to be all right," he told her, resting a hand on her slender back. "If it's still there and alive, we'll help it."

Rain started to fall as they strode out the front door and across the lawn. When they were far enough away from the house, Dragos shapeshifted, expanding in size rapidly until Pia shrank in his perspective to the size of a doll. The dragon bent his head to her. She touched his muzzle, a quick, affectionate gesture, and then he scooped her up to nestle her in a secure cage of his claws and launched into the air.

When they had decided to leave the city and move upstate, Dragos had learned every detail of the back and side roads of his new terrain. Well versed in the layout of the nearby town, he flew with exact precision to the street where Elizabeth Creedy had lived.

Once there, it took only a few moments to figure out the location of her street address. Within minutes the dragon touched down silently in the middle of the road in front of a small, well-kept craftsman-style house.

It was close to midnight, and the surrounding

neighborhood was mostly dark and quiet. Streetlamps provided regular sparks of illumination that highlighted spitting rain and newly formed puddles on slick asphalt. A few lights shone in windows, but Dragos felt certain there weren't any witnesses to their arrival. Setting Pia on her feet, he folded back his wings and shapeshifted back into his human form.

Pia gave him a mute glance. She was so obviously bracing herself to discover something grim and sad inside, he shook his head and plucked the Tupperware container out of her hand.

"You don't have to do this." He kept his voice quiet. "I can. Wait here."

"As much as I love you, I have to say, you're a scary sight to most people." She spoke as quietly as he did. Her eyes were huge shadows in her pale face. "Imagine how scary you'll be to one starving, scared dog."

"At this point, it might be scared enough of anything and inclined to bite," he told her. "I'll take care of it."

Plus, if the dog was in bad enough shape that it had to be put down, he could do that quickly without the added emotional distress it would cause Pia if she were present.

"Okay." She twisted her hands together. "Be gentle."

He nodded and strode up the walk to the dead woman's house. As he crossed the porch to the front door, the boards underneath his boots creaked. Hysterical barking erupted from deep inside the house.

He glanced back at Pia. That answered the main

question. The dog was in the house and still alive. And it was in decent enough shape to be energetic about intruders.

Grasping the doorknob, he broke the lock with one quick flex and eased inside. The smell of urine and feces assaulted his nose. Abruptly, the barking stopped. Dragos followed the telltale sounds of scrabbling until he reached a shadowed bedroom. His keen eyesight could see very well by the dim light of a nearby streetlamp. Miss Creedy had been tidy. The bed was made, the drawers and closets closed.

He could hear the stressed breathing and terrified heartbeat of the dog cowering underneath the bed. Going down on one knee, he infused his voice with Power.

"You're safe," he said. "Come out now."

It was a mundane creature. Normally, it wouldn't understand a total stranger who chose to carry on a conversation with it, but the magical compulsion in Dragos's words brought it out from underneath the bed. It stank. When he laid his hand on its shivering back, he could clearly feel its spine and ribcage underneath the tangled fur.

A quick scan told him several things. It was not a young dog, perhaps nine or ten years old. It weighed around twenty-five pounds but should weigh closer to thirty, but while it was suffering from hunger and stress, its underlying constitution was sound.

"Good dog," he told it. He set down the Tupperware

container and opened the lid. When he offered it a piece of bacon, the dog hung its head and refused to take it. "Eat."

More trembling underneath his hand. Timidly the dog took the bacon from his fingers. The taste must have triggered its appetite because it wolfed the piece down. Dragos offered another piece. This one was snatched out of his fingers and inhaled. He fed the dog a third piece. Then a fourth.

A soft footstep sounded behind him. Pia had slipped into the house. He said telepathically, *Could you bring some water?*

Of course.

Within moments, she stepped into the bedroom carrying a bowl of fresh water, which she set down beside Dragos's foot. The dog's trembling had increased at her presence. Moving the bowl closer to it, Dragos said, "Drink."

It obeyed, lunging at the water in ravenous gulps.

When it lifted its dripping muzzle from the bowl, Dragos said, "Good dog." He cast a sleep spell, and the dog folded onto the floor with an exhausted sigh.

Pia's voice sounded thick with unshed tears. "That was excruciating."

"It didn't want to eat. I had to compel it." Dragos straightened out of his crouch.

"I'm not surprised. It's scared to death." Pia moved to the doorway. "I'm going to turn on the light."

A moment later, light flooded the room. Together

they regarded the sleeping animal on the floor. Dragos said, "It really is the ugliest dog I've ever seen."

Pia tilted her head as she examined the dog more closely. "It's a he, not an it." She went to the bed where a crocheted throw lay folded at the foot. "This will smell like home. Hopefully that will be a comfort." Shaking it out, she knelt to wrap it around the sleeping dog.

"Right." He pulled out his phone. "I'll call animal control."

Pia rose to her feet and turned to face him. "Dragos Cuelebre, you'll do no such thing."

He paused with his phone halfway to his ear. "I won't?"

"We're taking him home with us."

An avalanche of reasons for why they shouldn't piled up in his mind. He said, "Pia—."

Raising her chin, she held up a stiffened finger. "I don't want to hear anything you have to say. This dog was loved by a good woman who was kind to our son. She's dead now, and you can keep him from pining to death and make him eat. We're taking him home tonight."

She had called him by his full name, and that stiffened finger meant business. Apparently, now was not the time to bring up the sex and the sleeping, and the indulgent breakfast that had been on his agenda before crossing over to Rhyacia.

Biting the insides of his cheeks, he kept his tone mild. "I see."

She knelt again to wrap the sleeping dog in the throw. "I'm so angry for not thinking of this sooner. The poor thing didn't have to go through the last three days."

"Go easy on yourself. It's not like you were close friends with Miss Creedy," he felt compelled to point out. "There were any number of people who knew her better and could also have thought of this sooner—like the principal at her school, and the other teachers."

"I know. That doesn't make it any easier. At least he didn't die, and we can help him now." She picked up the dog and stood. "Could you see if there's any dog food we can bring with us? It'll be better for him if he can eat the food he's used to, at least for the next week or so. Be sure to grab his bowls."

"All right." A quick search of the kitchen unearthed a bag of premium dry dog food along with several cans of wet. Tossing everything into a paper shopping bag, he joined her where she waited by the front door. "This should tide it over until we figure out what to do with it."

"It's a *him*, not an it!" She glowered, but his tact had its limits and he had no true remorse to offer. She sighed. "Okay, let's go home."

"Sounds good to me." He was all too glad to leave that place that smelled like abandonment and stress. Escorting her outside, he changed into the dragon, scooped her up, dog and all, and headed home.

The rain came down in earnest now, and was threatening to turn into an outright storm, with lightning flickering in the distance. While his tough dragon's hide provided all the shelter he needed, the woman and the dog he carried couldn't repel the weather quite so easily. He shielded them as best he could with both front paws, and after he had landed on their front lawn and shapeshifted back into a man, he scooped the dog out of her arms, and they ran for shelter.

Once inside, she headed for the kitchen and he followed. She turned brisk and businesslike. "Please put him on the counter."

"He's filthy."

Her blue eyes flashed, but her tone remained patient. "I know he is. Put him on the counter anyway. It can be cleaned later. I want to trim off that tangled fur while he's quiet. You can keep him asleep for me, can't you?"

"Of course." Dragos laid the animal on the counter.

"Thank you, my love." She reached up to give him a kiss, and some of his crankiness faded. "I'm going to make you a drink. Do you want coffee, tea, or brandy?"

One of the fascinating aspects of mating and marriage was the infinite complexity and variety of their communication with each other. On the surface, Pia simply asked if he wanted a drink, but in reality what she communicated was more nuanced.

He took a moment to puzzle it out. Right now, she was both praising him for helping to rescue the dog and soothing his irritability at thwarting his attempt to foist the dog onto someone else.

Was she placating him because she was apologetic?

No, that went too far. She had drawn a line, and she wasn't sorry about it. But she *was* offering to reward him for letting her have her way.

Communicating with her could be every bit as complicated as dealing with inter-demesne relations. It also had the added bonus of being much more enjoyable. Pleased that he was (almost) certain he had figured it all out, he replied mildly, "I'll take a brandy."

She smiled. "Keep an eye on him until I get back, okay?"

"Sure." Laying his hand on the dog's torso, he scanned to make sure it was still deeply asleep.

Within moments, she returned with his brandy and a pair of scissors, and as he took a seat at the kitchen table, she unwrapped the sleeping dog and trimmed around its muzzle and face. After that, she lifted its tail to clip the hair around its rear end. Sipping his brandy, he watched her work.

After a moment, she remarked, "His collar says his name is Skeeter. I think he might be a cockapoo? With maybe another breed mixed in. He has the bones of a good haircut. She must have had him groomed, maybe six weeks ago. He's definitely due for another one. And of course, he had an incontinence problem in the house, poor baby."

The brandy was one of his favorites and slid down his throat like golden fire. Casually, he offered, "I can hire someone to look after it full time, you know."

Her blue gaze lifted from the dog, and she looked at

him from underneath lowered brows. He returned her regard with a bland stare of his own. Pia wasn't the only one who could say several things with one statement.

"Him." Her tone had turned implacable. "Not it."

Pinching the bridge of his nose, he had to concede that point. "Him."

She turned back to her job. After she finished grooming the dog, she picked him up to lay him gently on the floor. Then she swept the clippings into the trash bin, cleaned the scissors and the countertop with disinfectant, and washed her hands. Clearly, her mind was busy at work on something. "We got Liam a puppy. Maybe we should have one for Niall too."

"Liam took responsibility for his dog," Dragos pointed out. "Niall is still just a baby."

There was a wall clearly visible in those beautiful blue eyes of hers, and it was swiftly growing to a width and breadth that rivaled the Wall of China. "Niall might grow every bit as quickly as Liam did."

"Niall hasn't yet shown us what he's capable of. Plus, the last thing we need is for him to stab the dog or set him on fire."

"He wouldn't," Pia said with conviction. "We wouldn't let him." She filled one bowl with water, and the other with dog food. "We can't keep Skeeter unconscious forever. You need to get him to eat and drink a bit more, then take him out."

"I am not calling any creature Skeeter," Dragos said. "And how did looking after him suddenly become my responsibility?"

Pia scowled. "He has lost his person and his home, and he hasn't eaten for three days. You can keep him calm, and you can encourage him to eat and drink, so you can get him through the worst of the changes he has to face when he wakes up."

She might have a point, but that didn't mean he had to like it. "Fine," he snapped. "We're still leaving for Rhyacia in the morning."

"I didn't say we weren't, my love." As she reached up to kiss him, the front doorbell rang. Her scowl returned. "Who could that be at this time of night?" Dragos spun toward the hall, but she caught his arm before he could escape. "You take care of Skeeter. I'll go answer it."

She was not going to let him off the hook. He growled, "Fine."

"Thank you," she murmured softly.

Damn it. Every time she used that tone of voice, he turned into a sucker. This woman had more power over him than anything else on earth. Succumbing to the inevitable, he gave her a swift kiss then turned his attention to his current albatross.

Crouching, he waked the dog gently. It still needed a bath, but it smelled better now that Pia had given it a hygiene trim. As it sat up, he infused his words with Power again as he murmured, "Be calm." Whining, the dog licked his hand and shivered. He cupped the side of its head. It was too small and stringy to consider as a snack. "Eat, drink. All is well."

When the dog obeyed, Dragos kept most of his attention on Pia as she answered the door. Not that he was concerned. While they enjoyed a great deal of privacy in the evenings, they did not live alone. Guards, the house staff, and groundskeepers resided in various buildings all around them. And besides, Dragos had erected his own wards all over the property. If whoever stood on their front doorstep meant to do them harm, he felt certain he would know about it.

Still, anyone knocking on their door in the middle of the night had a story to tell, and chances were good that the story would not be a usual one. He heard the hinges of the door creak as Pia opened it.

The fresh, wet scent of rain blew down the hall and into the kitchen, along with the astonishment in Pia's voice. "Aryal! Niniane?"

"Pia!" Niniane exclaimed. "It's so good to see you! I was afraid you might have left for Rhyacia before I could get here."

Aryal and Niniane were here?

Niniane was a little slip of a Dark Fae woman who used to go by the nickname Tricks. She had lived as a refugee in his demesne (when it had been his demesne) for many years. Now, she had taken her rightful place as Queen of the Dark Fae and ruled in the Other land of Adriyel. Tiago, who had once been one of Dragos's Wyr sentinels, had mated with her and left New York to go live with her.

The dog had finished gulping down its meal. Dragos

strode to the kitchen door, opened it, and ordered, "Out. Do your business."

The dog dashed out. Dragos barely paid attention. He was focused on the conversation going on at the front of the house.

Adriyel was some distance away, with crossover passageways that connected it to Chicago. Niniane and Aryal arriving together was not such an outlandish proposition, since they'd once been thick as thieves, but what was Niniane doing here? And why had she come without Tiago?

There was a shuffle of footsteps on the hardwood floor, and a rustle of clothing. Dragos's imagination suggested hugging and such.

"It's wonderful to see you!" Pia said. "But what are you doing here?"

Niniane giggled—or sobbed?—and said, "I've decided to go with you."

"What?" Pia said.

Aryal snapped, "*You what?*"

Out on the lawn, Skeeter had taken care of his business with remarkable promptness. He must have had to go for some time. Dragos snapped his fingers at the dog. "Inside. Now."

Lifting its leg one last time, Skeeter dashed into the kitchen. Dragos shut the door and strode to the front of the house, the dog at his heels.

It was just as he suspected. The arrivals on their front doorstep had a story to tell.

Chapter Three

"WHAT?" PIA FELT stuck on repeat. She stared at the two women on her doorstep.

Niniane stood around five feet tall, and her build was slight enough that the harpy could carry her in flight. Like Dragos and Pia, Niniane and Aryal had been caught in the rain, only they'd had farther to fly.

They were both drenched. Niniane carried a backpack on one slender shoulder. Her silken black hair lay plastered against her forehead, emphasizing the angular structure of her small face, the large gray eyes, and revealing her pointed ears. Her energy was odd, clenched and opaque, as if she was cloaking her Power in some way. While Pia took note of it, she didn't understand what it meant.

Aryal glared at the little faerie. "All you said was that you wanted to see Pia," she snapped. "You didn't say anything about going to Rhyacia. Does Tiago know about this? The way he was relaxing with the others at the bar, I'm betting he doesn't."

Niniane's shoulders crept up, and she gave Aryal an apologetic smile. "He'll figure it out when I don't come back. Right?"

"What the hell, Tricks?" Aryal said, her expression firing with real anger. "You're *leaving* him? Is that any way to treat the man who changed his entire fucking life for you—who *mated* with you?"

Niniane's expression grew appalled. "No, no—you misunderstood. I'm not leaving him! I'm leaving Adriyel, and I haven't figured out how to tell Tiago yet. I'm hoping I'll know what to say by the time he catches up."

The harpy didn't look placated. "Oh, so you decided to change your life without talking to him first? And he's supposed to just go along with whatever you dictate? Fuck that. Just… fuck the *fuck* out of that. Nobody should treat their mate that way."

Aryal might have a point, but her confrontational style left a lot to be desired.

"I think that's enough for the moment," Pia interjected, as she stood back from the doorway to gesture them inside. Flying was intense physical work. She knew from experience that Aryal would be starving. "Why don't you both come inside and dry off? I'll make some hot drinks and pull a snack together, and then we can talk."

"That sounds good!" Niniane exclaimed. Her teeth were beginning to chatter. "D-doesn't that sound good, Aryal?" Her gaze shifted away from the angry harpy to the hallway behind Pia, and a glimmer of real pleasure lightened her tense features. "Dragos, hi! Wow…did you get a dog?"

"No, I did not," Dragos said. "We rescued it earlier this evening. Pia's right. You can explain what's going on after you come in and dry off."

"Okay! Shall I use one of the guest bathrooms on the left?" With a leery sidelong look at Aryal, Niniane dashed up the stairs.

"Screw you, faerie," Aryal muttered angrily. "I'm calling Tiago."

When she pulled her cell phone out of her jeans pocket, Dragos executed one of those maneuvers that demonstrated how fast he really was. Reaching around Pia, he plucked the cell phone out of Aryal's hand. "Go dry off," he ordered. "Calm down."

The harpy glared at him, looking as mad as a wet cat. "You're not the boss of me anymore. Remember, you quit that job. Give me back my fucking phone."

Smooth as a shark cruising in shallow water, Dragos glided past Pia. As he did so, he flattened one hand on her chest and pushed her behind him, carefully. His powerful body had turned seamless with aggression, and the tiny hairs at the back of Pia's neck rose in instinctive response.

He said, his voice soft, "Make me."

Shadowing his heels, Skeeter growled at Aryal.

"Cut it out!" Pia ordered. She'd been talking to the dog, but when both Dragos and Aryal paused to look at her, she decided to take advantage. Pointing at them both. "You predators have the worst tempers of anybody I've ever met."

Actually, Aryal had the worst temper of anybody she'd ever met—harpies were famous for their tumultuous, often violent temperaments—but Dragos wasn't known for his sunny demeanor either.

"Make him give me back my fucking phone, Pia," Aryal said, her expression obdurate.

"You can have your fucking phone back when Dragos says you can," Pia told her. "Niniane is clearly struggling with something. Remember that you love her, give her a break, and when she feels safe enough to talk about it, she will. Now, my baby is asleep upstairs, and I want him to stay that way. You can either come in and behave yourself, and have something to eat, or you can head back to New York right now."

As she spoke a glimmer of sanity crept into Aryal's stormy gaze. "Uh… I guess I'll have something to eat."

"You know where the kitchen is." Pia stepped to one side. As Aryal shouldered past them, Pia looked at Dragos. Somewhere in the middle of her little speech, his own anger had eased. He looked at her with his eyelids half closed, a small smile tugging at the corners of his mouth. She shrugged impatiently. "What?"

"I love it when you get dictatorial," he murmured. Hooking one arm around her waist, he pulled her close for a deep kiss.

Holy gods, he was impossible to resist when he decided to turn on the sexy. Melting against him, she hooked one arm around his neck as he slipped the tip of his tongue—just the tip—between her lips. He made a nearly inaudible sound of frustration.

If she didn't put on the brakes now, she didn't know if she could stop. Pulling back, she searched his face. *What's going on with you?* she asked telepathically. *You seem unusually grouchy this evening.*

Reluctant humor gleamed in his hot gold gaze. *Don't mind me. I'm just feeling cockblocked. By this time of night, I had expected us to be on round two of sex. This would have been the slow round, with my head between your legs. The one where I don't stop, no matter how you might scream or beg.*

Oh wow, she said stupidly. A wave of heat washed over her, like smoke from the dragon's breath curling around her body, and an empty hunger liquified between her legs. *That sounds amazing.*

The heat in his scrutiny intensified until it sizzled the air. He slipped one hand between her thighs to cup her. *You okay there, lover?*

He was never one for sweet talk or endearments, except, occasionally, that one. She tried to clear her throat, and it came out a whine. *I—I'm not sure I am.*

"Hey, you guys mind if I eat this bacon in the fridge?" Aryal shouted.

The hand between her thighs clenched into a fist. Dragos made that nearly inaudible noise again, a frustrated growl so quiet it was just a vibration. Pulling away, Pia clapped both hands over her mouth and snorted with laughter.

Aryal strode into the hall, carrying the Tupperware container. She shook the container at them. "Bacon?"

Still hanging out at Dragos's heels, Skeeter barked. Dragos closed his eyes. He looked like he was in real pain. "S-sure." Pia tried to keep her voice from wobbling. "Go right ahead."

"Awesome. There's also some kind of casserole thingy. I had a bite. It's delish."

Pia waved her hand. "You might as well."

"Thanks." The harpy wandered back into the kitchen.

"And there goes the breakfast part of the agenda," Dragos muttered, making her laugh harder.

Sensing movement at the top of the stairs, she sobered. Niniane came down. She was drier, not quite so manic, but the strange cloak still dampened her energy. "Are you okay, honey?"

"I'm pregnant." Niniane dropped the cloaking and burst into tears. Suddenly Pia could sense it and smell it in her changed scent.

Dragos said, "Oh shit."

Niniane wailed louder.

A WHILE LATER, they sat at the kitchen table. Niniane's story had come out punctuated with great honking sobs.

She had been drinking a lot lately.

("Because, why not?")

The pressure of being the Dark Fae Queen was unrelenting. She spent a lot of time thinking about what could've or might've been.

("The old coulda, woulda, shoulda," she said with a

sad hiccup.)

Then, one night, she'd stopped blocking the possibility of a pregnancy.

("I was drunk, there was no excuse, and I dropped the birth control spell for a night. It was like poking holes in a condom. Let's see what happens, I thought. Probably nothing's going to happen in a single night. I mean, I know Wyr males have mighty, irresistible sperm, but Tiago would have been blocking things on his end too. Right? I just… I felt so tired. That's not an excuse. I'm not making an excuse. I'm just saying that I'm tired of pretending to be single, even though everybody and their grandmother knows Tiago and I are lovers. But to the Dark Fae, having a Wyr for a lover is like having a dirty secret. To them it's a perversion, it isn't something we're supposed to talk about, and I was tired of everything and everyone. And when I reached for Tiago that night, I wanted to pretend and forget.")

Pia sat with her arm around the smaller woman's shoulders, listening to the outpouring of pain. Dragos sat at one end of the kitchen table, turned sideways in his chair, arms folded and frowning into space. Skeeter lay with his head on Dragos's shoe.

Aryal's belligerence had completely disappeared. At one point she left the room quietly and was gone for several minutes. When she returned, she leaned against the doorway at the edge of the room.

Niniane rested her head on her forearms, refusing to look anybody in the eye. "So the way I see it, I can have an abortion and go back to Adriyel like nothing's happened," she said dully. "Or I can have the baby in secret, give it up and go back to Adriyel like nothing's happened."

Covering her mouth with one hand, Pia met Dragos's gaze then closed her eyes. The pain involved in those two choices was terrible to contemplate.

"Or I can have the baby openly, declare it my heir, and make it a target for assassination attempts its entire life, because the Dark Fae are xenophobic, racist shits, and gods forbid that a half-breed of any kind lay claim to their precious shitty throne." Niniane took an unsteady breath. "Or I can abdicate and have the baby…and still make it a target for assassination attempts its entire life, because it will have a legitimate claim to the throne, and gods forbid *that* would ever happen. And I don't know how to tell Tiago. I did not behave well that night, and it's easy to tell someone you love about something you're proud of. It's lot harder to tell them something you're ashamed of."

Aryal stirred. "That's okay, you don't have to tell him. I already did."

Niniane's head shot up. "You *what?*"

The harpy looked unrepentant. "I went upstairs, borrowed Eva's cell phone, and called Tiago. He's going to be here in the next half hour. He's really mad, but he might calm down some by the time he gets here."

"I can't even look at you right now!" Niniane exclaimed.

"Oh, come on, I did you a favor. You just said you didn't know how to tell him. Problem solved. You're welcome. You never should have kept him out of it to begin with."

"It wasn't any of your business!"

Aryal opened her eyes wide. "I'm standing right here, aren't I? You made it my business when you asked me to fly you two hours north."

Niniane roared, "THAT'S NOT THE SAME THING, YOU JACKASS!"

As the two broke into an impassioned argument, Pia pinched the bridge of her nose and closed her eyes. She said telepathically to Dragos, *Does Aryal ever do anything she's actually supposed to do?*

Right now, I'm having a tough time remembering anything.

Remind me to never tell her anything in confidence.

Aryal has her strengths. She's a relentless investigator, and there is nobody more loyal, vicious, or creative thinking in a battle, but she's a disaster when it comes to interpersonal matters. If you need to be reminded of that, then you're in a lot more trouble than either of us can help. He pulled out Aryal's cell phone, crushed it in one fist and set the mangled piece on the table.

Aryal's mouth dropped open in outrage. She snapped, "Oh, thanks so much for nothing, Dragos."

Dragos met Pia's gaze. *Why are we still awake?*

She bit her lips, because smiling was the exact wrong thing to do right then. Taking Niniane's hand between hers, she said, "Aryal shouldn't have done that, and when Tiago gets here, you and he will have a lot to discuss. I want you to know, I am your ally no matter what you decide to do. You've been under an unbelievable amount of stress for years. And if you and Tiago decide you want to come to Rhyacia…" She glanced at Dragos, who gave her a subtle nod. "We'll welcome you with open arms. You'll be safe, you'll have time to decide whatever you need to do, and we'll have your back no matter what. Nobody's going to hurt anybody's baby on our watch."

"Y-you promise?" Niniane looked from her to Dragos.

Dragos shook his head. "Nobody."

Niniane's face crumpled and deep sobs wracked her slender frame. Pia gathered her into her arms, while Aryal watched with her mouth turned down like she might cry too.

Pia said telepathically to Dragos, *And we're taking Skeeter with us too.*

He rolled his eyes. *Of course we are.*

Outside the storm grew worse. Lightning struck several times in quick succession. Ironically, a look of relief washed over Niniane's exhausted face. "He's almost here," she said. "Wow, he really is mad."

"That's our cue," Dragos said to Pia. She stood when he did. He said to Aryal, "You—out."

She gave him an incredulous look. "What? Why me?"

He said between his teeth, "Give. Them. Some.

Privacy. You cretin."

"Fine, I'll go home," she snapped. "Thank you for everything you did, Aryal—said nobody."

"Oh my God," Niniane cried. "Leave by the back door, before you can cause any more damage."

Dragos snapped his fingers at the dog. "Outside. Do your business."

Skeeter jumped to obey. As Aryal went out with them, she asked, "Are you sure he isn't your dog?"

"He is a rejected snack," Dragos said.

"But you're good with him. Maybe he *should* be your dog."

Dragos snapped, "The only pets I kept were sentinels, and you were all pains in my ass."

Pia could not laugh. She couldn't, not in the face of Niniane's agonized anticipation. Gently, she asked, "Do you need someone to sit with you until Tiago gets here?"

"No," Niniane said, although she looked like she wanted to say otherwise. "That's okay. I created this mess. It's mine to fix. Tiago and I will figure things out."

Kissing her cheek, Pia said, "The guest room at the end of the hall is yours if you want it. If you're going to leave, don't leave without saying goodbye, okay? One way or another, let us know how things go."

"I will. Thank you for everything." Niniane hugged her tight.

Pia didn't wait for Dragos. She wanted to be out of the way when Tiago arrived, so she headed for bed. Eva sat at the top of the stairs, elbows on her knees while she turned her cell phone over and over in her hands. She was a beautiful woman, with brown skin, bold, sensual features, and the muscled body of a fighter. Niall's baby monitor lay on the floor beside her.

Baby monitors. That was another thing they would have to rethink in Rhyacia.

As Pia picked up the monitor and sat beside her, Eva gave her an apologetic glance. "I had no idea that harpy meant to do evil when she borrowed my phone."

"Of course, you didn't." Pia watched Eva flip the phone between her long fingers. The action woke the home screen up, and she caught a glimpse of a familiar, young Elven woman with blue-tipped hair and a mischievous smile. She recognized the woman straight away. It was Linwe, one of Beluviel's most devoted Elven attendants.

A lightbulb went off. Oh. *Ooooohhh.* Maybe Eva had a crush on Linwe.

Keeping her tone casual, she asked, "Remember when we traveled down to Charleston to the Elven demesne? I was pregnant with Liam and I had to pee every five minutes."

"How could I forget?" Eva scratched her jaw, smiling. "I hated your guts back then."

"You got over it." She leaned affectionately against Eva's arm. "That was back when we first met Linwe, wasn't it? Wasn't she part of the escort that took us into Beluviel's Wood?"

Eva stopped spinning her phone, covered the screen

with one palm, and looked at Pia sidelong. "Might have been."

At the time, Eva had been head of the security detail charged with protecting Pia on her first diplomatic trip to another demesne. Pia said, even more casually, "You know Linwe went to Rhyacia with Bel, right?"

"Yeah. So?"

She shrugged. "Maybe you should ask her out when we get there."

The skin of Eva's cheeks darkened as she laughed a little under her breath. "Ask her out to what, go see a movie? Rhyacia isn't really a place to go dating right now."

Pia was sure she had hit a nerve. She pressed, "There are plenty of things you could do. You could ask her to go for a hike, or to go hunting…" Not that Pia could ever think something as horrible as hunting down and killing another creature could be a date, but this wasn't about her. "The lake where we're building the city is huge. Dragos flew me over it once. There are several beautiful beaches. You could ask her out on a picnic and go swimming."

She'd halfway expected Eva to grin and say *hubba hubba*, or something else about enjoying a hot woman in a bikini. Instead, Eva frowned down at her hands. "I'm not sure it's a good idea to get involved with someone who has such different loyalties."

Ooooooohh. Maybe there was more going on than just a simple crush.

"Oh, come on," Pia said after a moment. "Look at Niniane and Tiago. Rune and Carling. Graydon and Beluviel. Hell, look at me and Dragos. People from different races, different Wyr natures, and different demesnes make relationships work all the time. Besides, you'd just be asking her out on a date. There would be plenty of time to figure out anything else if things turned serious."

And it would be no bad thing for Eva to consider dating someone like Linwe, who had already demonstrated the capacity for deep loyalty and commitment. When Wyr mated, they did so for life, which could be a dangerous proposition, especially if that Wyr mated with someone of a different race. Now was not an appropriate time to bring that up, but Pia made the observation, and she approved.

"It might be a moot point anyway," Eva said. "I haven't asked her to do anything."

"No, you haven't, but you should. Because if you don't ask, you know the answer is no. If you do ask, the answer just might be yes." Dragos appeared at the foot of the stairs, Skeeter at his heels, and Pia stood. "That's my cue. Thanks for watching Niall."

"No problem." Eva stood too and kissed her cheek. "See you in the morning."

Dragos nodded at Eva as he passed her on the steps. When he reached Pia, he said levelly, "We don't have a doghouse."

"Oh for God's sake," she exploded. "Scrub that

thought from your mind. Skeeter is a house pet. We're not putting him in a doghouse."

"This whole situation is very wrong." He gave her the same kind of fierce frown that had once frightened most of the inhabitants of Cuelebre Tower. Hell, it had once frightened her.

As they talked, Skeeter sat. The adoring expression in the dog's eyes as he watched Dragos made a weird feeling flutter like a butterfly around in her chest. "That's okay, honey," she crooned, patting Dragos's arm. "You'll adjust. For tonight, he's sleeping with us."

"Oh no." Total rejection flashed across his face. "No."

"On the floor," she added quickly.

"Why do you insist on tormenting me like this?" he demanded.

"Tiago is going to barge through our front door at any moment," she reminded him. "And we can't just shut Skeeter in another room. Come on, it'll be fine."

Taking him by the hand, she led him into their bedroom. He threaded his fingers through hers. "Just think, a couple of hours ago I was a happily married man."

"Ouch!" she said laughingly.

"I wasn't done." He squeezed her hand. "I had just retired. Life was so simple."

She pulled away, dropped the baby monitor on the bed, and gathered up the throw they kept at the foot of their bed. Folding it, she told him, "Life is still simple.

You are still happy, and your wife is both hot and wise."

"She is. I will grant you that," he said, eyes gleaming.

"Now there's just a dog on your floor, so quit being a big baby and let's go to bed." She set the folded throw on the floor and stood back to admire her handiwork. It was probably a good thing that the throw would smell like them.

Dragos snapped his fingers at Skeeter. "Go to bed." Skeeter curled up on the throw and looked at Dragos soulfully. Dragos sighed and clenched his jaw. Then he said, "Good dog."

The dog sighed too and closed his eyes.

Pia said with heartfelt sincerity to Dragos, "I have never loved you as much as I love you right now."

"Woman, you are a complete mystery to me," he told her, even as he pulled her into his arms.

"I know," she said gently, laying one hand against his cheek.

He glanced at the clock and then out the French windows where predawn had begun to light the horizon. "Maybe we have time for one round before Niall's next feeding. What do you think?"

"That sounds great to me." As he lowered his head, Niall started to cry. Skeeter leaped upright and started barking.

"What the actual fuck," Dragos said. She had never seen him look so offended.

Pia bent at the waist and laughed so hard tears sprang to her eyes. She choked out, "It's not his fault. He didn't know there was a baby."

"*Stop*," Dragos ordered. Skeeter cut off in mid-bark but looked extremely alert. Dragos looked at Pia. "I'm not getting sex tonight, am I?"

She laughed harder. "At this rate, I'm not sure we're getting any sleep either."

When she turned to go to the nursery, Dragos caught her by the wrist. "Make yourself comfortable. I'll get him."

"Thank you." As she stripped down, she watched him stride out of the room. The dog sprang to follow.

A few moments later, she heard Dragos murmuring over the baby monitor, "Quit making such a fuss, Stinkpot. You'll get your titty juice in just a moment."

Titty juice? Clapping both hands over her mouth, she fought to remain quiet so she could hear what happened next.

Rustling noises. He was changing the baby's diaper.

Excited barking.

Thumps, curses, more barking. The scrabble of hooves and paws. The brittle sound of something breaking. Oops, that must have been the lamp beside Niall's changing table.

Then, "Oh for fuck's sake, Niall—it's just a dog. Cut it out. No, you can't stab it! Change back, goddammit!"

She lost her struggle for self-control in an explosive guffaw.

Chapter Four

S TINKPOT WAS EVERY bit as fast as his father. He had two big advantages. He was only twelve pounds, so he could turn on a dime, and his strategy was pure chaos. What he couldn't do was outthink his father's experienced wiliness. After a few minutes of scrambling, Dragos had the little shit scooped up and firmly tucked underneath his arm. The baby's four hooves paddled the air as if he were still running.

"Calm down," he told the dog as he grabbed a fresh diaper. Obediently, Skeeter stopped barking and followed him back to the bedroom. There, Dragos found Pia red-faced with laughter. As soon as Stinkpot saw his mother, he started paddling faster as if that could get him to her more quickly.

"Change back now, sweet baby," she said as she gathered him up. As soon as he was in her arms, Niall abandoned his Wyr form and eagerly latched onto the nipple she offered. Within moments peace reigned in the room.

Dragos shed his clothing and stretched out on the bed beside his mate and child. These were some of the times he treasured the most, the quiet of the room, the luminous love that Pia radiated, the delicate baby gradually falling asleep as he nursed at her breast.

It filled him, those moments, in a way that nothing had ever filled him before, not war and killing, not even sex and mating. Peace poured into his cranky old soul.

He stretched out on his side, facing them, and rested one hand on Pia's flat abdomen. When, after a few minutes, Skeeter sneakily crept onto the foot of the bed and rested his head on Dragos's ankle, he chose to let it go.

What did it matter, after all? The dog's life was nothing more than a fleeting moment, and he had already lived most of it. He should have what comfort he could for the short time he was here.

Dragos didn't quite sleep, but he rested and dozed as the sun came up. He knew the moment Tiago had stormed into the house, and one part of him took note of the intense rise and fall in Tiago and Niniane's conversation. Eventually, two sets of quiet footsteps came up the stairs and traveled down the hall to one of the guest rooms.

Beside him, Pia finished nursing Niall. She eased the baby onto his back on the mattress between them, and her breathing grew deep and regular. Dragos allowed himself another hour of rest. Then he eased off the bed, showered, and pulled on a pair of jeans.

Skeeter waited and watched by the bathroom doorway. Dragos snapped his fingers at the dog and went downstairs. He fed Skeeter and let him out to do his business, made coffee, and texted the house staff to bring a large breakfast buffet, with a generous selection of fresh fruit, chocolate vegan muffins, a tofu scramble, and a large assortment of meat and eggs. Pia needed the vegan selections, and Tiago was very nearly the same size as Dragos, and his appetite was just as capacious.

While he waited for the house staff to bring breakfast, he drank coffee and watched the news on the flatscreen that occupied one corner of the spacious kitchen. He had propped the back door open, and fresh air and sunshine spilled into the room. They had left the old throw on the floor, and Skeeter grabbed it with his teeth and dragged it over to Dragos's feet, then dug it into a pile, turned around three times, and settled down on top of it.

Tiago was first to enter the kitchen. A powerfully built man with dark brown skin, black hair, and harsh aquiline features reminiscent of American Indian ancestry, he had a typically impassive demeanor, but his Power cracked around him, filled with thunder and lightning. He was still dealing with some intense, tumultuous emotions.

Thank the gods it wasn't one of the women, because then Dragos would have to talk about their feelings. And Pia was the only woman whose feelings he was truly interested in.

Tiago nodded to him on the way to the coffee. As he poured himself a mug, Dragos asked, "So, are you coming with us?"

"For now," Tiago replied. "I sent word back to Aubrey in Adriyel that we're going to take an extended vacation. Aubrey will handle the rest. We are having the baby. Nothing else has been decided."

Dragos nodded. None of that surprised him.

And that was it. He and Tiago had just carried on a lengthy conversation, for them. Tiago took a seat at the kitchen table. They watched the news and drank coffee.

After ten minutes or so, Tiago said, "Aryal said you got a dog."

Dragos opened his mouth to say, no I didn't, but oh, why bother? He shrugged in disgust.

Soon the house staff arrived and set up the breakfast buffet in the dining room. While they worked, Pia appeared dressed in jeans and a T-shirt and carrying Niall on her chest in a baby carrier. Niall was still in his human form and sleeping. Pia's tired expression brightened as she took in the expansive spread of food.

"I prefer your cooking," Dragos told her. "But Aryal ate the entire casserole last night."

"Thank you for arranging this." She kissed him, and then turned to greet Tiago.

They elected not to wait for Niniane since, as Tiago said, she had worn herself out the night before. While they ate, Eva arrived and helped herself to food. Now that the time had come, Dragos asked Pia, "When do you want to leave?"

She studied Tiago, who shrugged. "You shouldn't

wait for us. I want the faerie to sleep until she wakes up on her own. We can always follow when we are ready."

Pia nodded. "Then I think we should leave right away. There's nothing else keeping us here. We're packed, we're ready. We just have to figure out how we're going to transport the dog."

"There's nothing to figure out," Dragos replied. "He flipped out when he met Stinkpot in his Wyr form. God knows how he would handle the dragon. I'm going to make him go to sleep."

Tiago remarked laconically, "I can't believe you got a dog."

"For fuck's sake," Dragos muttered underneath his breath. Pia's eyes danced.

After that, it was a simple matter of carrying their personal luggage outside. Most of their things had been sent ahead. They had five backpacks, one for each of them, and one for the dog's food they had taken from Miss Creedy's house. Pia would carry Niall in his baby carrier on her chest and wear her backpack. Eva would carry the sleeping dog strapped to her chest and wear her backpack. Both women would keep their hands free just in case. Dragos would carry the rest.

They went outside, Dragos shapeshifted into the dragon, and they arranged themselves accordingly, the two women riding astride high on his back, where his neck met his shoulders. Dragos launched, feeling a lightness he hadn't felt in a very long time.

The first stop was at the guard station that had been

built at the entry to the crossover passageway. Dragos had spared no expense on creating the borders to Rhyacia, and he shapeshifted back into his human form so he could conduct a quick inspection. Eva watched the baby and the dog, while Pia accompanied him.

This station was their first line of defense against anyone who might potentially want to invade Rhyacia. Troops would be stationed here on permanent assignment, with several experienced magic users. There were barracks and customs offices, along with a state-of-the-art security system and weaponry. There was barbed wire atop a high wall, and they had ground-to-air missile capability.

Eva was an experienced soldier and took it all in stride, but Pia hadn't seen the crossover passageway since the station had been built. She stared at everything silently, her face pale.

He waited.

After a moment, she said, "I guess the other two crossover passageways have similar guard stations?"

"Correct." His voice was hard. "Nobody is getting onto my land without my say-so."

He would do all of this and more to keep Pia safe, but it wasn't just about her anymore. Niall bore the same Wyr form that she did, and there were creatures in the world who would do anything and pay any amount of money, would go to war and bankrupt nations, just to get ahold of one of them.

She stared off, her head turned away. He waited a

few moments more.

In a whisper, she asked, "Do you ever regret… any of this?"

Rage like lightning whited out his mind. How could she ask him that? Because he was so angry, he moved with care when he took her shoulders and turned her to face him. The sadness in her expression kept him from shouting, and he remembered that, even though she was a more than competent fighter, unlike him she was a creature of peace at heart. So for her sake, he curbed his temper.

"Never once," he whispered through his teeth. "Never, on any day for the rest of my very long life, could I regret any of this. In fact, if it were possible, I would choose it all over again. If I could, it would be my extreme pleasure to hunt down and kill anyone who might even potentially think of doing harm to you and our son." Her expression lightened, and when that happened, he found that his anger did too. He added, "And we're having sex tonight, goddammit."

The last of her odd sadness broke apart as she laughed.

And there it was, that moment, with happiness dancing in her aquamarine gaze and the air around her effervescent with her Power—that moment was what the dragon would do anything and kill anyone for.

That moment was what he lived for.

That one, and then the one after that, and the one after that, all grouped together in his mind like luminous pearls on a string. Each one came to him new, a perpetual gift of joyful surprise, and as rich as he was, and as many jewels as he'd acquired, those moments were the sum total of the dragon's true treasure.

THERE WAS ANOTHER guard station on the Rhyacian side of the crossover passageway, and Dragos wanted to inspect that one as well.

This time, when Pia accompanied him, she had questions. "Why is this station designed differently than the other one?"

Instead of answering, he asked her a question. "What are the potential capabilities of any enemies who attack the Earth-side station?"

"That's easy. They are on Earth so they can attack with both technology and magic." She frowned. "And even though they can come at the crossover passageway from several different directions, they have only a small entryway, because if you don't hit a crossover passage-way just right you don't actually enter the passage."

"Correct. And what about here?"

"This is the exact opposite. They can only come out of the exit of the passage, which is one narrowly defined area."

"Also correct," he said. "And if you know you can only have a few people coming through that narrow space at any given time, who would you put first?"

Her gaze narrowed. "I would put the nastiest magic users I could find through first. Because technology won't work on this end, so guns have no use here. And they have to be mobile, so they can't use heavier war machines like trebuchets. They need to move as quickly as possible, with as much missile capability as they can throw." She glanced sidelong at him. "Flaming arrows?"

"Absolutely flaming arrows. And morningstar spells, and panic spells, and some of those bastards will try cloaking themselves to go undetected. So, on this side of the passage, we load up on magic users, and we keep the newcomers contained. When they come in—not that they are ever going to get this far—they have to learn the terrain fast, but we don't want to give them any clues. My magic users can be stationed at several different levels behind these high concrete walls. They are protected, while they can throw spells and shoot arrows through the slits there, and there." He pointed.

"You've created a kill box," she said, staring at the giant oval wall that surrounded the land of the passageway. There was only one set of metal reinforced doors. The only two ways out of the kill box were to go back through the passageway to Earth, or to take wing and fly.

He paused. "First off, I'm rather impressed that you know the term kill box."

"I used to watch TV, you know," she confided. "I looove Jack Ryan."

He laughed. "I know you do. Yes, this is a kill box. The chances of it ever being needed are probably one in a million, but if that one chance happens, we'll be ready."

"Remind me to never piss you off."

He kissed her swiftly. "You could never piss me off that much. Do you want to see the rest of the station?"

"Oh, no. I've had enough of looking at murder places now. I'll be ready to go whenever you are. Just remember, that baby has been sleeping for a few hours, and he's going to wake up at some point."

"I have a few questions for the station commander, but I'll make it quick." Her expression made him pause. "What is it?"

"You know, anybody who would want to launch an attack against us is probably going to know how the odds will be stacked against them in this situation." Her gaze was both clear-eyed and sober.

He frowned. "What's your point?"

"If I were that person, I wouldn't launch an overt assault that would be expensive and probably doomed to fail." Her smile twisted. "I would want to send someone in secret, someone who could pass the checkpoints and get through customs, because they look innocent and normal, and they would appear to have legitimate business. Maybe someone who everybody thinks of as a friend."

A chill passed down his neck. "You mean an assassin."

She searched his gaze. "Am I wrong?"

He shook his head. "That's what I would do, so no, you're not wrong. I'm just saddened—and again impressed—that you realized that."

"He's my child too," she whispered.

He put his hand on her shoulder. "We're going to be in a more sheltered environment overall, but that doesn't mean we'll relax our vigilance. There are two levels of stations, and they are populated by the smartest, most capable people I could find. We will also continue to have guards in the city where we live, along with personal guards. And just as soon as Niall is big enough, we're going to train that boy how to stab things really well."

A grim kind of hilarity entered her sharp gaze. "He's going to love it."

"Yes, I think he will." He squeezed her shoulder. "Give me two minutes, and then we'll head for home."

"Okay."

He located Malan Wei, the station commander, soon enough. She was a tough, experienced soldier with a long record of exemplary service in the Wyr demesne. Her Wyr form was one of the nastiest Dragos had ever encountered, a giant, spider-like creature called a Jorogumo. She had a poisonous bite and could move like lightning.

To a Wyr of Dragos's strength and size, her poison was akin to a mosquito bite or bee sting, but for the gryphons it could cause temporary paralysis. For any creature smaller, it could even cause death. Malan could have easily been a contender for a sentinel position, except she didn't want to interact so intensely with the civilian population. The position of station commander suited her to perfection.

Malan greeted him cheerfully and provided him with the budget report he'd requested. She also gave him a packet of correspondence from the build site that had accumulated since the last package had been delivered to their house in New York. He shuffled through the letters. Nothing looked urgent, so after meeting with Malan for a few moments, he took his leave.

When he rejoined Eva and Pia, he saw they were in luck—the baby had not yet awakened. After shape-shifting back into his dragon form, the women climbed astride, and they embarked on the last leg of their journey.

The air quality was impeccable. In Rhyacia, it was late morning, and the sun had yet to banish the last of the morning's coolness. The dragon breathed deeply, feeling himself expand, as the beating of his giant wings echoed the rhythm of his heart. There were no power lines, no aircraft, no cities, no frantic vehicles roaring down paved highways.

There was just the land scrolling underneath the wide, immaculate sky. While they weren't within eyesight, mountains to the north remained snowcapped through the seasons. He flew down the coastline of the immense lake to the south, where palm trees and brilliantly colored birds of paradise proliferated, and the bromeliad that some humans called Spanish moss dripped from ancient oaks and cypress trees.

A sprawling settlement of tents, Quonset huts and

other prefab houses hugged the coastline, crisscrossed with dirt paths. The settlement neighbored the construction site of the new city, which was located at the foot of a massive granite bluff, the top of which would be the location of his and Pia's new home. Dragos had missed the penthouse in Cuelebre Tower. He wanted height and the ability to gaze out over miles of blue water and land.

As they approached their new home, the women exclaimed in excitement. Pia asked him to fly lower, and he obliged. On the ground, he could see tiny figures of people pointing up at him. More ran out of tents and buildings, and their combined voices rose in jubilant welcome.

After long weeks of anticipation, the Lord of the Wyr and his mate had arrived home.

Chapter Five

FIRST OF ALL, when Niall woke up, he didn't notice or care where he was. He just wanted to run and run and run and run and run, blithely oblivious to the locale, common sense, or any reason.

Pia managed to keep hold of him until she could get him down the path from their temporary house to the private stretch of beach Dragos had cordoned off for their personal use. When she set the baby down, he exploded into his Wyr form.

As he careened with haphazard joy down the beach, Pia and Eva chased after him for a good hour to make sure he didn't hurt himself before he finally slowed down and agreed to change back into the baby to be fed.

Secondly, when Pia had heard they would be staying in temporary housing until their permanent home was finished enough to occupy, she'd been picturing something primitive like an army-style tent with composting bucket toilets and camp showers out the back.

She couldn't have been further from the truth. After feeding Niall on the beach, she and Eva returned to the house at an easy jog. Dragos and Skeeter had disappeared, no doubt so that Dragos could talk to the dozens of construction foremen and settlement officials who had gathered to clamor for his attention.

There was no lack of work to be done and, Eva told her, there were already close to twenty thousand souls present. Everything in the city was growing at once. There were representatives from mundane human governments and all the Elder Races present—Elves, Vampyres (currently at rest), other Nightkind, and witches, and Demonkind, and both Light and Dark Fae—from countries and demesnes all over the world.

Several embassies were already in the process of being built, and while each person present in Rhyacia had passed a rigorous security inspection, a Wyr police force maintained a smiling presence throughout the settlement. The citizens of the world continued to consider Dragos a premiere force to be reckoned with, no matter how remote his locale.

With Dragos gone, that left Pia to explore their temporary living quarters at her leisure. Their prefab house had been positioned in such a way that it was surrounded by other dwellings occupied by security and house staff, but the area had been landscaped to provide them with a screen of foliage for privacy. Eva's cottage was tucked into one corner of the square.

The entire compound had been gated with a high privacy fence and felt like a small, self-contained village. Before he left, Dragos had told her that the compound even had a convenience store located inside the gate with fresh produce, a selection of cheeses, wines and other liquor, candies, baked goods, hot stir-fried foods, and other amenities. If she needed or wanted anything, all she had to do was send a request and it would be delivered.

Once inside, Pia discovered their house was an eighteen-hundred-square-foot living space with three bedrooms, vaulted ceilings, large windows, two fireplaces—one in the living room and another in the master bedroom—two and a half bathrooms, and a kitchen with soft-close drawers and polished granite countertops.

Comfortable, stylish furniture decorated the living room. There were hand-woven rugs. There were several bookshelves filled with Pia's favorite genres of fiction and a carefully curated selection of nonfiction that neither she nor Dragos had yet read. The bedroom beside the master had been decorated and furnished with Niall's things that she'd shipped ahead two weeks ago. Dressers and the closet in the master suite were filled with her and Dragos's clothes, all clean and neatly pressed and folded.

Sliding glass doors in the master suite led to a private deck furnished with more comfortable furniture. The kitchen had a capacious pantry filled with canned, dried, and shelf-stable foods. There was a walk-in insulated ice box with a selection of fresh and raw meat, eggs, butter, and both vegan and omnivore prepared foods. Large fresh blocks of ice kept the box cold.

Testing the kitchen faucets, she discovered hot and cold running water. Ceiling fans spun lazily in the rooms, moving the warm air in a pleasant way.

Niall had fallen asleep again, and while he was still a small baby, she had been carrying him for most of the day. She tucked him into the crib in the nursery with a sense of relief.

Can I interrupt you for a moment? she asked Dragos telepathically.

Most people with telepathic ability had a range of about ten feet or so. Dragos's range was closer to a hundred miles. He replied immediately, *Of course.*

This house is quite a surprise, she told him. *And the books! You never said a word about any of this.*

It's a bit small, but I wanted it to be comfortable. Some people are fine with roughing it in tents for now, but no mate of mine who gave birth two months ago is going to live in a tent. And you've got enough on your plate just looking after our hellspawn.

She snorted out a laugh. Only Dragos could think an eighteen-hundred-square-foot house was small. *I love everything about it, but I'm curious… The ice is being shipped down from the mountains, and solar panels on the water tank are heating the water, right?*

Correct.

So, what's powering the ceiling fans?

There are four small wind turbines on the roof. As wind turns the turbines, it propels the fans. There's usually a good breeze coming off the water, so they should keep moving, but if there's a significant lull in the wind they'll slow down and stop. If the fans are too much, you can always slow them down or turn them off by using the switch panels located by the doors.

You are such a tech geek. She smiled as she said it. Then, because she couldn't resist, she added, *This place is outstanding, and the path leads right down to the beach. Are you sure we shouldn't just live here?*

His reaction was immediate and satisfying. *I would go nuts if I lived in that house indefinitely. I need more space. I'll have offices down here in the city, but I need one at home as well. And you need your own space too. And we need room to entertain, whenever we're ready to do that, and we also need guest suites. And since we don't have cars or a public transport system, we have to provide comfortable housing for house staff and security.*

Halfway through, she started laughing. *I'm only teasing. I happen to think this place is magnificent, and I love it, but I know you wouldn't be okay here forever.*

I'm glad you love it. I wanted you to be happy. And it will do for even a year or two if we need it that long.

They talked for a few minutes longer, but he had grown distracted, which was a sure sign that people were interrupting him in person, so Pia said goodbye. Eva had left to settle into her space. There was nothing to do, and nowhere Pia needed to go. She could have called for Jocasta or Ramone, the Wyr couple they had hired for house staff, so they could babysit while she went swimming or exploring.

But she had also gotten perhaps an hour's nap the night before, and she wanted to revel privately in the luxury of being in her new home-for-now. This wasn't a vacation, she reminded herself. She had all the time in the world to explore later. Plucking a paperback off one bookshelf, she settled onto the large, comfortable couch and began to read. It was a great story, by a favorite author. Six pages in, she fell fast asleep.

A quiet knock brought her leaping off the couch. First chance she got, she needed to make a sign that said BABY SLEEPING. Setting her book aside on the couch cushion, she rushed to answer the door.

Graydon's mate Beluviel stood on the doorstep a miniscule newborn strapped to her chest, Linwe by her side. The beautiful Elven woman looked happier than Pia had ever seen her. Pia exclaimed in delight when she saw the baby girl's downy head. "It's so good to see you—and you brought Giselle!" She hugged the other women. "Niall's asleep. We have a sitting area on a deck. Would you like to sit outside? And please tell me I can hold that little girl."

"Of course, you can." Beaming, Bel transferred the baby into Pia's arms. "I'm so glad you've arrived. I do love new beginnings, but the whole settlement is in chaos, and there's building dust everywhere. Trust me, you don't want to go out in the afternoons. Your house is wonderful."

"Dragos thinks it's too small." Pia rolled her eyes and laughed. She smiled at Linwe. The younger Elven woman carried a bow and quiver on her back and had dyed the tips of her hair bright pink. Casually, she said, "Linwe, you look great. Eva's going to be glad to see you."

Linwe's eyes brightened. "Is she here?"

Ooooooohhhh. Was it possible Eva's feelings were reciprocated?

Pia pointed out Eva's cottage. "She is, and that's her cottage right there. Why don't you let her know you and Bel have come to visit?"

"Be happy to." Linwe took off with a saucy sway of her hips.

Pia rounded her eyes at Bel, but she couldn't say anything outright, because she didn't want to speak out of turn. She settled on saying, "It would be *so* good for those two to see each other more often."

A knowing smile deepened in Bel's ageless green eyes. "I couldn't agree more. Linwe works too hard."

"Eva does too." Pia cuddled Giselle. The baby was much smaller than Niall. Every tiny feature was pure perfection. "Can you stay for a visit? Then they can go on down to the beach if they like."

"I think that sounds perfect."

When the other two women arrived, Bel and Pia worked together to send them off. Eva's normal poise deserted her, and she got a deer-in-the-headlights look in her eyes. Linwe watched Eva sidelong, a tiny smile playing around the edges of her lips. When they finally disappeared, Pia had to wait until she was sure they were out of earshot.

Then she grinned at Bel. "Oh, I feel good about that."

Bel laughed. "I do too. It will be interesting to see what they do with themselves."

"I don't want to give your baby back." Reluctantly, Pia handed Giselle back to her eager mother. "If you'd like to go out to the deck, I'll get us some drinks."

"I'd love to."

Pia dug through cabinets for glasses and poured some of the fresh cold tea she found in the icebox. Foraging further, she found light coconut cookies. Since she was the one in the household with a sweet tooth, she knew those would be vegan, and she arranged some on a plate. Then she carried the refreshments out to the deck to visit with one of her favorite people in the world.

When she had first met Beluviel, she had felt an immediate accord with the other woman. Bel had been Lady of the Wood in the Elven demesne just outside Charleston, and she was one of the few people who knew Pia's Wyr nature. Since then, so much had changed. Bel's husband had been killed, and she and Graydon—another one of Pia's favorite people—had fallen in love and mated.

"I can't tell you how good it is to be here, and to know that you're here too," Bel told her.

"I feel the same," Pia confessed, sharing a smile of conspiratorial delight with the other woman. "Tell me everything that's been going on. According to the time in New York, you and Graydon left yesterday."

Since time didn't flow in Other lands the way that it did on Earth, the inhabitants of each Other land experienced time slippage in some form or another. In Rhyacia, time flowed more quickly—sometimes faster and at other times a little less fast, making it impossible to calculate the exact difference.

Bel replied, "We've been here three days, and in many ways, I really love it. There's too much going on at once, which makes things feel chaotic at times. But there is so much happiness in almost everybody you meet."

"That's good," Pia murmured, relishing the Elven woman's bright presence and the dappled sunlight falling through the trees. The first generation of the Elder Races carried tremendous Power, and Beluviel shone against her mind's eye like a star.

"There are also factions and arguments already."

"What? People have been here for like five minutes."

"I know. The Dark Fae are feuding with the Vampyres, and the Light Fae group have managed to bribe some of the construction workers off one of the city buildings they were working on. The foreman of the city building is threatening to bring charges against the workers that abandoned her project."

"How can she bring charges when Dragos hasn't finalized the law structure?" Pia frowned. For the moment, Dragos's word was the only law Rhyacia had— and by extension that authority would also be Graydon's.

"Well, exactly," Bel said. "Nothing's going to come of it, and she's got to know that. I think she just doesn't want to get penalized for not meeting her deadlines. Oh—and the Demonkind have set up a distillery too close to some living quarters. There've been multiple complaints about the smell, along with some drunken brawling, and…and just don't let any of them get to you. If anybody tries to approach you with a grievance, send them to Graydon. He said to make sure to tell you that."

Graydon had centuries of experience with being one of Dragos's original sentinels in New York, and he was well versed in handling civil, personal, and criminal disputes. Dragos had already asked him if he could consider becoming governor of the city, and while Graydon hadn't yet officially replied, the general expectation was that he would probably accept.

"Got it," Pia replied. "Sending grievances to Graydon won't be a problem." She had more than enough experience with people trying to get to Dragos through her, and the tactic annoyed her to no end.

"And listen to this." Bel leaned forward, her expression turning intense. "What I really wanted to come over to tell you is, there are stories circulating about possessions that have gone missing from one place, only to be found somewhere else. And it all appears to be random. There's quite a shopping market, with all kinds of stalls—we should go sometime—and a shopkeeper told me when he'd gone back to his tent one evening, he found his mattress high up in a nearby tree. Nobody saw anything. Tools have gone missing from construction sites and were later found scattered on the beach. Some people think there's a thief, and others believe it's a prankster, but nobody sees anything when it happens. Nobody can figure out who it is, or how they do it. They're calling it *the unseen*."

"How strange." Pia frowned. "If it was a prankster, you would think with so many Wyr around, they could catch the person's scent."

"I know. And Pia, it's already happened to us. I'm always careful with the things Gray gives me. He's not a very—let's say, he's not a very possessions-oriented man, if that makes sense. So, when he gives me something, it carries a great deal of meaning. Last December, he gave me a beautiful Masque present of two silver and emerald hair combs."

"I remember them. They're really gorgeous, and they suit you."

Bel smiled. "I wear them all the time, and I'm careful where I put them. Two nights ago, I set them on my bedside table. The next morning, they were gone."

"Oh, no!"

"It's all right—I found them again. We have a prefab house too, about a quarter of a mile away at the edge of the forest. The combs were on our front doorstep."

A slow chill moved across Pia's skin. "Are you saying that somebody came *into your house* while you and Gray were sleeping and took your combs?"

Bel's expression had turned sober. "I'm saying that I put them down on the bedside table one night. We slept soundly. And the next morning they were on our front doorstep. Gray went out of his mind."

"I would think so," Pia murmured. "Did either of

you find anything?"

"No scent, no sign of entry, nothing else missing, no vandalism. I sensed nothing. He sensed nothing. He even brought some of the most experienced magic users into the house. They couldn't find anything. All they could say was it must have been the unseen."

"That's really creepy." Pia rubbed her arms. She thought of Niall, asleep in the nursery, and felt an almost overwhelming urge to go check on him. "Have any people gone missing?"

"Thankfully, no. But—listen to this—there's also been trouble at one of the construction sites."

"What kind of trouble?"

"It's not vandalism, or at least right now nobody thinks it is. It's the site of the future concert hall. Every time they get the frame of the hall erected past a certain point, it collapses. They've gone through three builders with three different attempts. They've had dowsers check for hidden weaknesses in the land and found nothing. The site appears to be solid, and the plans have been checked multiple times for design flaws. Nobody can figure out why they can't build a building on that site."

Pia couldn't sit still any longer. "Excuse me for a moment. I have to check on Niall."

"Of course."

She was too sensible to rush. But she did enter the house briskly and slip into the nursery as quietly as possible. Her heart pounded as she approached the crib.

Sprawled on his back, Niall snored peacefully, one

fat fist pressed against the side of his head. Suddenly she could breathe again.

She rested a light finger on his fat, warm little belly. Precious hellspawn.

Then she found she couldn't walk away, not after listening to the stories Bel had told. Not after knowing that something, somehow, had slipped undetected past one of the most sensitive and magical Elves Pia had ever met, along with one of Dragos's most Powerful sentinels, to steal something off Bel's bedside table. No wonder Graydon had gone ballistic.

Bel had said nobody had going missing, but still. Anything that had the strength to transport a mattress up into a tree could easily whisk away a baby.

Gathering up her sleeping son, she held Niall close and buried her nose in her son's soft, sweet neck. As she inhaled his scent, something delicate and almost indetectable brushed against her awareness.

A quiet thump sounded somewhere in the empty house.

Adrenaline surged like a mule's kick. She shot out of the nursery, through the master bedroom and onto the deck. At the same time, she screamed telepathically, *Dragos, I need you!*

Where are you? His reply was filled with a universe of calm.

On the outside d-deck with Bel.

On my way.

Bel had leaped to her feet, Giselle tucked into the

baby carrier at her chest. "What is it? What happened?"

Pia couldn't talk. She was shaking all over.

Within moments, a gigantic bronze meteor plummeted from the sky. The dragon landed with a crash that took out several trees, his great eyes glowing volcanic gold. A somewhat smaller golden meteor landed beside him. It was a gryphon: Graydon. A third meteor arrived. It was some kind of winged creature. Pia didn't recognize who it was and didn't care. She kept her attention trained on Dragos.

The dragon shapeshifted into the man, and Dragos raced toward her. He took hold of her upper arms even as he scanned the area with a sharp gaze. His Power was raised to such an extent she could hardly bear to stand near him; he radiated so much heat.

"You're shaking like a leaf." His voice was hard. "What happened?"

"There was something in the house." Her lips had gone numb.

He turned a killer's face to the sliding glass doors. Graydon had shapeshifted into his human form as well, conferring softly with Bel. The third winged Wyr had shapeshifted into a male with a soldier's tough demeanor, crow's feet radiating from the corners of his eyes and streaks of gray in his sandy hair.

"Wait here," Dragos told her. He opened the sliding glass doors and slipped into the house.

"Paul, stay and guard the women," Graydon said. He didn't wait for an acknowledgement and slipped after

Dragos. The unfamiliar male stood alert, watching everything.

Eva and Linwe erupted from the path to the beach and raced toward them. "We saw the dragon. What happened?" Eva asked sharply. Linwe had run to Bel and Giselle.

Pia shook her head. At the moment she couldn't speak. She was still shaking. Unbelievably, Niall still slept through all of it.

A few moments later, Dragos and Graydon stepped out of the house. Dragos flattened a hand on Pia's back. "We didn't find anything," he told her quietly. His gold gaze was sharp with concern.

"There was something," she whispered.

"Do you know what it was?"

She shook her head. "Something."

The stranger spoke up with an easygoing smile. "Could it have just perhaps been the wind? Maybe no reason to panic or call 911."

Dragos's killer expression snapped back over his face, but Pia forestalled him by digging her nails into his forearm. She didn't feel quite grounded in her body. She said through gritted teeth, "I don't know who you are, but it's none of your fucking business if I panic every day for the next fifteen years and scream for my husband. And he will come every time, because you know why? I have been kidnapped more than once. I have been shot at. More. Than. Once. I have been shot. So, if this is your condescending attempt to de-escalate a hysterical woman, you can get the fuck out of my life right now. Go away."

As she spoke, it wiped the patronizing expression off his face. He paled. Looking at Dragos, he said apologetically, "My Lord…"

"Addressing me instead of responding directly to my mate is your second mistake," Dragos growled. "Pia told you to leave."

The man's face clenched. Bowing, he backed away and strode off.

The tableau on the deck pulsed with tension: Graydon with Bel and their baby. Linwe had her bow drawn, an arrow fitted into place and pointed at the deck. Eva, on one side of Pia, and Dragos on the other, while her beautiful disaster baby slept through it all.

Then, even though it was difficult, Pia turned to Eva. "Please take Niall."

"Of course," Eva murmured. She gathered up the baby and held him protectively.

Pia looked at Dragos. "Let's walk through the house."

"I was going to suggest that." He looked at Graydon. "Are you coming?"

"Hell yeah."

Pia stepped inside, followed by the two men. Dragos kept a hand on her shoulder. It didn't stop her from shaking, but she felt slightly better at the physical connection. "I felt something," she said. "I don't know what it was."

"I know you did," Dragos said. "How does our bedroom look to you? Is it how you last left it? Study everything."

She took a long careful look. "It looks fine. I heard something from the other side of the house."

"We'll still take it room by room." His voice was calm and reassuring.

It unlocked her panic enough so that she could turn toward him. "It was like…" She held a hand an inch or so over his forearm without touching him. "I'm not making contact, but do you feel that, whatever that is? The warmth from my hand, my energy, whatever you want to call it."

"Yes." The killer in his gaze turned analytical.

She passed her hand over his forearm. "It was like that. Like I felt something walking past me. It didn't quite touch me, just like I'm not quite touching you. But I felt it."

"Okay, got it. Let's check the next room."

Taking their time, they walked through the house. Neither male had weapons drawn, but their combined raised Power told her they were ready for anything.

And they found nothing. Nothing. Nothing. Not in Niall's nursery. Not in any of the bathrooms or the other bedroom. Not in the kitchen.

At last they stood in the living room. Pia rubbed her forehead, feeling a headache coming on. "I don't know what to say," she said at last. "I know what I felt. And I know what I heard."

"We believe you, cupcake," Graydon told her. "There's been some weird shit going on here."

"I was going to tell you about it when I got back," Dragos murmured.

"Bel already did," she told him. "And I got to thinking, if something could move all that stuff around, it could move a small baby pretty easily too."

Dragos looked grim. "Understood. Whatever it was, it appears to have gone for now. Unless you still feel something?"

As she shook her head, her gaze fell on the paperback on the floor by the couch. A chill ran along the back of her neck again. "That's what the thump was," she said. "The book."

"What do you mean?"

She walked over to the couch, picked up the paperback, and set it firmly in the middle of the seat cushion on the couch. "This is where I left it when I went to answer the door. I remember I set it down deliberately on the seat cushion, because sometimes things can slip off the arm and I wanted to keep it quiet because Niall was napping. This paperback is far too heavy for the ceiling fan to have blown it onto the floor, and it didn't leap off the couch on its own." She lifted her gaze to meet Dragos's. "Something was in this house. I felt it go past me. And it knocked the book onto the floor."

Chapter Six

CAREFULLY DRAGOS TOOK the paperback from Pia. Grasping it by one corner, he held it up to his nose. Pia's scent clung to the pages, and, more faintly, he caught Jocasta's scent. Jocasta and Ramone were the ones who had unpacked and arranged everything in the house.

He could sense no lingering magic, and no other information of any kind. It was simply a paperback book.

He handed it to Graydon, who inspected it as carefully as he had. Then both males went over every inch of the room. They didn't find anything, but by that point Dragos had expected nothing else. It was still important that they check. No information was still data to be used for analysis.

While they inspected the area, Pia sat in one of the chairs, leaning forward to rest her elbows on her knees and burying her face in her hands. Graydon gave Dragos a troubled look, then he signaled his intention to step out by tilting his head in the direction toward the deck and left.

Dragos squatted in front of Pia and contemplated

the dejected slump of her shoulders.

She peered over her fingers at him. "I have PTSD."

Cupping one of her elbows, he nodded. "At this point, I would expect nothing else."

"Did I overreact? Of all the things we've faced since we've gotten together, we've never had something invade our living space. It completely freaked me out."

She was entitled to feel everything she felt and behave in any way she wanted. He didn't care if she had overreacted, but he knew she did. She liked to behave in a fair and balanced manner. After giving it some thought, he replied, "I don't think so. Something unknown and not understood came into our home uninvited. And Paul was out of line."

"Who is he, anyway?"

He shrugged that off. "The city police captain." Or at least he had been. Some of the older predator Wyr held chauvinistic attitudes toward herbivores, and Dragos had every intention of firing him when he got the chance. "I want you to consider taking Niall back to New York for now."

At that, she lifted her head to give him a long, level look. She asked evenly, "Are you quite certain that's what you really want?"

The way she asked made him reconsider his own words. Scowling, he clenched his hands into fists. If she returned to New York, it would mean a bigger separation than they had ever faced before.

And staying in New York would be no guarantee

that she and the baby would be safe. He would not be able to see personally to their protection. If something happened to them, he wouldn't find out about it for days, and from the look in her eyes, she had already realized that. She was just waiting for him to come to the same conclusion.

"No," he growled. "What if you and Niall went to stay at the guard station with Malan?"

She raised one eyebrow and waited patiently.

He thought through that one too. Again, if something happened to them, he would not find out about it for hours. He hissed, "Damn it."

Gently, she said, "What you really want is for us to remain close by and safe. Now that I've had a chance to calm down, I'm not sure we were in any danger." At that, he started to speak, but she rested fingers against his lips. "I'm not sure we weren't either. My bottom line is, we absolutely need to do everything possible to protect the baby. I propose we stay as long as we keep alert eyes on him at all times. If whatever that power is could slip past Bel and Gray, it might be able to slip past even you. And we don't know if it would hurt a child, but we don't know that it wouldn't. Until we find out more, we don't take any chances."

As she spoke Graydon and Bel, carrying Giselle and Niall, walked into the living room. Bel said, "I agree one hundred percent. No baby should be unattended until we find out for sure that the unseen won't hurt them."

Graydon handed Niall over to Dragos as he added,

"And, believe it or not, we've just had something of a breakthrough. Pia is the first person we've found who has sensed anything. We should see what else she might be able to discover."

Dragos's eyes narrowed. Like Pia, he had been in reaction mode and hadn't yet come to that realization. "Good point." He looked at his mate. "Are you willing to play detective?"

"Absolutely," she said at once. "As long as we go overboard about protection for Niall. I want full-on neurotic, Dragos. I'm ready to face any and all adventures and problems we may encounter, but I can't bear the thought of anything happening to the baby."

They'd had many discussions about security since they'd mated, and, if anything, Pia had been the voice for sanity. Otherwise Dragos would have her constantly surrounded with half a dozen guards at any given time. The fact that she gave him permission to go overboard filled him with immense satisfaction.

"Full-on neurotic it is," he said with a fierce smile.

THE FOUR SETTLED in the living room to discuss options. In the end, they decided that whenever Pia and Dragos chose to investigate, Bel and Graydon could keep the babies with them. Bel's Elven attendants provided a constant guard presence at the perimeter of their property, for whatever good that would do. Eva and Linwe could also take shifts to maintain eyes on both babies at all times.

Tiago and Niniane arrived while they were in mid-discussion. After greeting everyone and getting updated on current events, they offered to help guard the babies. In the end, even Pia had to agree they couldn't have found a more Powerful or capable babysitting team if they'd tried.

While they strategized, Eva and Linwe left to retrieve the dog that Dragos had left with others when Pia had called for help. When the women returned, Skeeter bolted to Dragos and leaned against his leg.

"I can't believe you got a dog," Linwe said, smiling. "It doesn't seem like you."

"I know, right?" Niniane exclaimed. "I couldn't believe it either."

As Dragos opened his mouth to strenuously deny it *yet again*, he caught a glimpse of the hilarity dancing in Pia's expression. Her return to laughter was so welcome he rolled his eyes but decided not to respond.

Instead, he said telepathically to Graydon, *Pia won't let me hire someone full-time to look after it.*

The Gryphon's expression was suffused with repressed amusement. *She won't?*

He glowered. *I do not live the kind of lifestyle that allows for looking after live snacks.*

That is actually an excellent point, Graydon conceded. *You already had to leave him behind once. Maybe he just needs to stay home based.*

Please hire a dog walker for him. Someone who is willing to be available 24/7. He paused. *They must love dogs. I think they should be open to adopting him.*

Graydon covered his face with one large hand. *Help me out here, Dragos. How is that different from hiring someone to look after Skeeter full time?*

His eyes narrowed. He didn't appreciate being laughed at. *Clearly I need to plan a guerilla campaign over this issue. It's all about a difference in terminology. Professionals hire dog walkers all the time. Surely not even Pia can object to that. Gradually, maybe it can sleep over at the dog walker's house now and then.* He rolled one wide shoulder restlessly. *Then we'll have it sleep over more often.*

I hate to tell you this, but I don't think that'll be guerilla enough. She's going to see you coming a mile away. The other male shook his head. *It would be a lot simpler if you just ask Jocasta and Ramone to watch him when you're not at home.*

Dragos growled under his breath. The dog had smelled of anxiety and stress ever since he'd entered the house. Putting a hand on Skeeter's head, Dragos said quietly, "Calm."

As the command took effect, Skeeter looked at him adoringly and rested his head on his knee.

The interaction did not go unnoted. "Look at that," Niniane exclaimed. "Aryal was right—you really are good with him."

"Right now, I am his Xanax," Dragos replied in a dry voice. "That is not a viable long-term situation for anybody."

"It's working for now," Pia said. "And we've got more urgent things to think about."

She had a point, and the conversation moved on. The others lingered and, since it had been such a long time since they'd all been together, Pia and Dragos invited them to stay for supper. It was good to relax with friends and old companions.

To Dragos's eye, even though Niniane threw herself into every subject and laughed often, she carried a kind of fragility, as if she were as breakable as glass, and Tiago watched her almost unceasingly. They had difficult decisions ahead of them.

If they chose to settle in Rhyacia, he wondered if Tiago might be interested in replacing Paul to head the police force in the city. He liked that idea. He liked it very much, but as Pia had pointed out before, people did not have to arrange their lives to suit him. Still, he would be ready to mention it should the situation arise where it might fall on welcome ears.

Over dinner, the group decided on a schedule for the next few days. Unless something unexpected happened, Pia and Dragos would take Niall over to Graydon and Bel's in the mornings to investigate the unseen.

Since they didn't know what they might uncover, it was impossible to plan too far in advance. To start with, they would retrace the scenes where items had been moved. Dragos also wanted to check out the construction site of the concert hall, although nobody knew if the two sets of phenomena were connected.

After everyone had said goodnight and left, and Jocasta and Ramone came to clean up for the evening,

Dragos settled Niall on his shoulder again, took Pia's hand and led her down to the beach.

The sunset threw a magnificent kaleidoscope of color across the water and sky. Niall shook himself alert, changed into his Wyr form and careened down the beach, kicking up his hooves and stabbing at rocks in the sand. Skeeter had already gotten used to Niall's shapeshifting and chased the baby, barking ecstatically.

When Niall whirled to point the tip of his horn at the dog, Dragos intervened. "*Niall,*" he said in a tone that brooked no argument. "*Do not.*"

Niall wavered. Swishing his tail, he regarded his father, while a hint of smoke curled out of one delicate nostril. There was such an assessing look in the little shit's eyes, Dragos fought a serious battle to keep from laughing.

"He is going to challenge you…," murmured Pia. Her complexion was reddened with the effort to hold back her own laughter. "I foresee years and years of challenges coming."

"I know," he murmured in reply. He repeated more loudly, "Do not stab the dog."

Niall broke from the contest of wills by tossing his head and cavorting away.

Dragos waited until the baby wore himself out and changed back into his human form. Then he said gently, "We have to talk again about binding him."

They had gone around and around on the subject before. Sometimes the Wyr faced the challenge of raising a child who was so strong and dangerous they had to cast a binding that would keep the child in its human form until it grew old enough to exercise self-control. Most commonly, the tactic was used on lion Wyr or other predators that might be inclined to violence.

Her expression darkened. "I hate the idea."

"I do too. But he's too strong willed and chaotic. If we don't bind him, at least sometimes, one of these days he's going to shapeshift at the wrong time, and his Wyr form will no longer be a secret." He paused. "I can protect both of you better here, but the danger of exposure is still very real. As soon as we decided to create a new society in Rhyacia, we allowed for that danger to exist. The only way we could have circumvented it is if we had come to live here by ourselves. And that kind of isolation wouldn't have offered a real life for any of us."

"No, I know." She picked up a handful of sand and let it sift through her fingers. "The situation never came up with Liam. He was too…"

"I think the word you might be looking for is sensible."

She laughed. "Maybe so. Also, we had no need to keep his dragon form a secret. Everybody expected you to have a dragon son. And even then, we still ran into problems, like the time when we went on vacation and he decided to climb out of the house and go on an adventure."

"Exactly." Watching her carefully, he suggested,

"Think of it like putting on a diaper. We already diaper Niall so he doesn't piss or shit all over the place. When he exercises enough self-control, we'll stop using the diapers. He'll still eliminate, but he'll do it when and where he's supposed to."

"And sometimes we can take the diaper off?"

He nodded. "We can take the binding off whenever he's in a safe enough place to allow him to shapeshift into his Wyr form, like here on this stretch of the beach. He'll still get the freedom to run and explore, only it'll be on our terms, not his. We can use it as a tool to teach him self-discipline."

She pinched the bridge of her nose. "Put like that, I don't think we've got any other real choice."

"I don't think we do."

"All right." It was clearly a hard concession for her to make, but the baby's safety had to come first, and as soon as Niall had shown an aptitude for early shapeshifting, they never really did have any other choice.

He pulled Pia between his legs and wrapped his arms around her. Holding the baby, she leaned back against his chest, and they watched the sun slip down past the horizon. The dog settled on the sand and leaned against his thigh.

Pressing his lips to the curve of her ear, he said, "About Paul."

Stirring, she said uncomfortably, "I really went off on him. I'm sorry."

"That's the last thing I want you to be. Yes, you went off on him, but he was inappropriate. Nobody behaves inappropriately to my mate and gets away with it. If you hadn't done it, I would have. In any case, that's not what I wanted to talk about."

"Okay," she said, her tone turning cautious. "What about Paul?"

He rested his cheek against her hair. "I don't think the woman I once met on Folly Beach in South Carolina would have been capable of doing what you did this afternoon."

She chuckled. "You mean the woman you hunted down on the beach."

With the wave of one hand, he brushed that off. "Semantics. I am making an important point here. Even as I started to respond to Paul, you stopped me and stepped in, and you gave him the dressing down he deserved. The woman I met on the beach had a mouth on her like I couldn't believe. She was feisty, and sexy, and endlessly fascinating. But I don't think she would have had the capability to do what you did so effortlessly earlier today. Sometimes when I look at you, I can see you still doubt yourself. You overthink things, and you worry constantly about whether or not you're doing the right thing."

"You're right," she muttered. "I do."

"On one hand, it shows you have a conscience." He tightened his arms. "But on the other hand, I wish you could trust yourself the way I trust you. I wish you could see how much you've grown, the way I can see it. You do the right thing more often than not, and when you don't, you're fluid enough that you're capable of executing a course correction and getting back on track. You have something. It's not just a moral compass, although it's that too. You have the ability to find your way in difficult circumstances, but it's also the ability to take command, to establish boundaries, and to back somebody off if they need to be backed off. I would like to see you to rely on that more. You are stronger and more capable than you believe, and I respect the hell out of you."

When he finished speaking, she was silent for so long he had just begun to wonder if he had said something wrong, then she whispered, "Thank you for saying that. It means a lot to me."

"I didn't say it to be touchy-feely." He was not a fan of touchy-feely moments. "I'm telling you the truth as I see it." He stirred. "Ready to go back up to the house?"

"Yes."

Since she had her arms full, he lifted her up effortlessly and set her on her feet. Within minutes, they had stepped back into the house. In the living room, Eva lay stretched out on one of the couches, reading one of Pia's paperbacks.

Followed by Skeeter, Dragos wandered into the kitchen to pull out leftover filet mignon from the icebox. While he stood at the counter and ate, he listened to the women talking in the other room.

Pia: "Are you sure you're okay with watching Niall tonight?"

Eva: "For the thousandth time, yes. I'm not sleepy in the slightest. All I did today was take a magic carpet ride on a dragon, which for me is like going to Six Flags. Then my best friend set me up on a date, and I went swimming with a gorgeous woman who has a saucy ass like you wouldn't believe."

Pia laughed. "I'm glad you had such a good time."

Eva: "After that, I took a walk with the same gorgeous woman to retrieve a dog—and that was cute, it was like another date—and then I got to have dinner with her. Being on assignment as your bodyguard has had some heavy moments, but I haven't even worked today. Quit fretting."

Pia: "I can't help it. You won't take your eyes off him?"

Eva: "I'll do even better. I'll keep him on my chest the entire time I'm with him. That little baby is going to get so spoiled. He's going to be held the entire time you're not with him. How's that?"

Dragos ate several bites of the beef while he listened with approval. That little baby was too young to have any sense. He should be spoiled rotten.

He caught sight of Skeeter sitting in a tight hunch in front of him, large dark eyes pleading. Really, the dog was quite ugly. He had a snaggletooth face, and Pia hadn't trimmed the hair around his eyes. It was sort of wavy and curly in places and brown, and it hung over his eyes.

Dragos remembered Pia had said Skeeter had been adopted. Who knew what kind of rough life the dog had lived, and most of that short life was already over. Had he ever tasted filet mignon?

"This is so inappropriate," Dragos muttered as he cut off a piece of the beef and held it out to the dog. "And it doesn't mean I like you."

Astonishment bulged in Skeeter's eyes. He lunged and inhaled, and the beef disappeared from Dragos's fingers.

For fuck's sake. The dog looked like Dragos had just hung the moon, and all over a stupid piece of beef. Dragos couldn't count the number of times he had eaten beef in his incredibly long life. This was pathetic. He cut off another piece and fed it to the dog, and then another.

A slight noise made him lift his gaze. Pia stared in astonishment.

"It doesn't mean anything," he growled. "I'm just feeding the rejected snack a snack."

She nodded. Holy gods, her eyes filled with tears. "Don't mind me." Her voice wobbled. "You know how emotional I've been since I've given birth. I'm going to take a quick shower now."

"Good," he said with more emphasis than he probably should have. Maybe that would give her a chance to calm down.

She disappeared down the hall, and as long as he lived, he would never understand women.

There was one more bite of beef left, half of it gristle. Dragos sneered at the thought of putting it in his mouth. But the dog rested his chin on Dragos's knee and looked like he might expire at any moment. He fed Skeeter the last bite.

On his way to the bedroom, he stopped to tell Eva, "Be sure to let me know if you get the slightest bit sleepy, and I'll take watch."

She half reclined on the couch, patting the baby's back as he lay on her chest. "Sure thing."

Maybe it was overkill. In all the stories he'd heard about the unseen, none of them had involved causing actual harm to anyone. There were other children in the settlement, and none of them had been taken. But Dragos was a big fan of overkill. Better to have overkill than to have something happen and agonize afterward about wondering if they could have done more to prevent it.

He strode down the hall to the master suite. Pia was still showering. Stripping off his clothes, he joined her. The shower stall was large and lined with travertine marble, with an oversized, square rain shower head that hung from the ceiling.

Water glistened on her rounded hips and graceful, violin-shaped back. She was soaping her hair and she paused to smile at him over her shoulder. His was a fiery nature, and desire burned through his veins to stiffen his cock.

Brushing her hands aside, he took over the task of

working shampoo through her hair, relishing the wet glide of his fingers through the soapy length. When he began to massage her scalp, she moaned and put a hand on the wall to brace herself. "That feels so good."

One corner of his mouth lifted. "It does to me too."

He finished washing her hair and moved to her shoulders, back, and breasts. Those he handled with extreme care, as she was breast feeding and they were often swollen and achy. He stroked the distended nipples and ran his fingers along the crease under the soft rounded globes, watching her expression as he worked his way down her body.

When he reached between her legs, she gasped and leaned back against the wall. "I don't know if I can stand up while you do that."

"Let's find out," he murmured.

She looked at him through lashes spiked with water. "Last time I ended up on the floor."

"See how long you can take it." He loved sex in the shower, and he had made sure their prefab had a shower big enough to accommodate both of them.

He loved the hot wet glide of their bodies moving together, loved the way she looked when she was drenched and lost in pleasure.

"I have a better idea," she said huskily.

She slid down to her knees in front of him, and he knew where this was going to go. Anticipation made him hard as a spike. She held her hand up, and he obliged her unspoken request by squirting liquid soap onto her palm.

Grasping his erection, she worked the soap all over it and the tight sac of his testicles underneath. She tightened her fingers, pumping him, and the pressure and cleverness of her touch quickly brought him to the edge of climax.

He gripped her wrists to pull her hands away, hissing, "Oh no, you don't. I don't want this to go that quick."

The reprieve he bought himself was all too brief. He had barely eased back from the edge when she leaned forward and took him in her mouth. So hot, so wet, so tight.

"Cocksucker!" he swore.

Exploding with laughter, she lost her hold on him. Grinning, he took the opportunity to go down on his knees. Angling into a sitting position, he urged her to climb onto his lap, and she swung one of her fabulous legs over his and came astride him.

That's it, that's what he wanted. He fingered her, growing serious, and watched her expression turn intense with need. "Come inside now," she gasped.

"Anything you want, lover," he murmured.

She positioned his cock while he held onto her hips, and when she eased down on him, he penetrated her, and it was exactly the right fit. They found exactly the right rhythm.

She clenched, he pumped, she wound her arms around his neck and clung, while he gripped her flexing torso and drove in harder. The rain shower poured and poured water over them, washing away everything from the day, the stress and anxiety from earlier when she had screamed his name and his entire world had stopped.

He clenched her too hard, crushing her against his chest so that she gasped, and even though he knew he did, he couldn't stop. Then his climax hit, a volcanic gush that shuddered through his body. Flexing throughout the pulsing pleasure, he lifted his head, eyes closed, and let the water pour over his face like tears.

He loved her, he loved her, but he was never entirely sure he knew what that meant. What was love, anyway?

All he knew was what she taught him day by day.

For him, love was a collection of moments like this.

Strung together like luminous pearls on a string.

Chapter Seven

NIALL WOKE UP after five hours. While Pia fed him, Dragos sent Eva back to her cottage to get some rest. Once the baby's appetite had been satiated and he had fallen back to sleep, Dragos settled him on his chest and took watch for the rest of the night.

They left early in the morning while it was still cool and relatively quiet. Dragos insisted Pia wear at least some protection. When she grumbled, he gave her a level look.

"Do we know what we're going to find when we investigate?"

She narrowed her eyes. "No."

"Precisely. We don't. That's why we're going to investigate. Is there the possibility we might run into something dangerous?"

"We probably won't, you know. This whole area was surveyed before we decided to develop here."

When Dragos decided upon something, his patience could be ruthless. He pressed. "When the area was surveyed, the engineers didn't know anything about the unseen. So is there the possibility that we might find something dangerous?"

"Fine." She glowered. "There is the possibility we might."

"If we are going to indulge ourselves in overkill, I want to see some of that indulgence spread in your direction," he said.

In the end she decided, with his approval, on wearing leather leggings and half armor that protected her torso. He strapped his sword to his back, and she chose to arm herself with a bow and a quiver full of arrows. It was the weapon she felt most comfortable with using. Her sword work was indifferent at best, and if for any outlandish reason they ended up in some kind of hand-to-hand conflict, she would do more harm by getting in the way. When Dragos fought he was an unstoppable juggernaut. Her best contribution was the accuracy of her aim.

They left the dog with Jocasta and Ramone. Pia had pumped breast milk for Niall, so when they dropped the baby off at Graydon and Bel's, they had several uninterrupted hours ahead of them.

He wanted to check out the site of the concert hall first, so that's where they headed. Construction had already begun in several different places, but the building dust had not yet gotten too irritating yet. Once at the site, Dragos found the foreman and asked a series of questions about what they had already tested for.

He was being thorough, but to Pia the conversation was all *blah blah blah*, so she wandered off to study the frame of the building that they had erected again. She didn't go far, and Dragos always kept her in his line of sight, but she did get enough distance so that their voices blended into the background.

The warm sunshine felt good on her exposed arms and face, and the breeze off the water felt refreshing. Opening her senses wide, she studied the beams, the cloudless blue sky overhead, and the raw ground that was strewn with building materials and tools.

When Dragos finally joined her, he asked, "Do you sense anything?"

She shrugged and shook her head. "It's nice here. How about you?"

He looked up at the sky. Dragos was the only person she had ever met who could stare directly at the sun. "There's something here," he said finally. "It's a feeling akin to a ley line or the kind of energy vortex you would find in Sedona. It's what attracted me to this spot in the first place—that, and the way the concert hall is positioned so that it should have some of the best views of the city and the harbor."

"But none of that should cause a problem with construction, right?" she said.

"Right. If we were on Earth, we could utilize technology to get some imaging of what might be going on deep underground, further down than we've gone to build the foundations here. There's something called an advanced ground penetrating radar system—GPR—that archaeologists have used to map out an entire buried Roman city in Italy without needing to excavate. I'd love to use that here."

She loved it when he talked geek, even if she tuned it out half the time. "You're sexy," she told him.

A masculine grin creased his face, even as he asked, "Does that add anything to this conversation?"

Lifting one shoulder, she muttered, "It adds to *my* conversation."

The sexual awareness in his gaze deepened. As he stepped closer, she knew she was about to be kissed. *Yippee ki-yay.*

Something brushed past her.

The hairs on the back of her neck rose. She spun, staring, eyes opened wide. There was nothing… There was….

There was the faintest, transparent outline of a tall figure walking past. She received a fleeting impression of flowing grace, an exquisite, inhuman face that turned to look at her, a grand curving shape that trailed behind, and radiant eyes.

"Did you see that?"

With the flex of one muscled arm, Dragos unsheathed his sword. "No. What is it?"

The frame of the concert hall listed. With a great yawning noise, it collapsed.

The figure had disappeared. She stared open mouthed at the rubble, then at Dragos. "It was magnificent."

Gripping his sword as if he wanted to cleave something in two, he snarled between his teeth, "*What was it?"*

He was the perfect killing machine. There was nothing more barbaric or splendid than he was when he got ready to do battle, but he had nothing to hit and no one to fight. She shook her head. "You might as well put your sword away, because it's gone."

Scowling, he snapped his sword back into its sheath. "Describe it."

"I barely caught a glimpse," she told him. "It was transparent, like you might expect a ghost to look on a TV show." That sounded lame, and she scowled as she struggled to find the right words. "It was as tall as you are, only more slender, and it had radiant eyes. And I think… I think it had wings. Dragos, I don't think we're alone here like we had first thought."

The foreman of the construction crew rushed up. He looked deeply distressed. "My lord, I am so very sorry this happened again. I don't know what we're doing wrong—we've tried everything we can think of—"

"You're going to stop building," Dragos told him.

The man stammered, "Of course, if that's what you think best—"

Dragos cut him off again. "Instead, I want you to clear this area and start digging. Something doesn't appear to want us building here, and I want to know if there's anything underneath this site."

"Yes, my lord. I think we can have it cleared enough to start digging this afternoon."

After that, they toured the rest of the settlement,

inspecting each site where the reports indicated that incidents had occurred, but they didn't discover anything else. Finally, they returned to Graydon and Bel's.

Tiago and Niniane had been taking babysitting duty, and after the six had gathered Dragos and Pia told the others what had happened. "Have any of you heard of a creature like this?" Dragos asked. "And why is Pia the only one who can see it?"

Bel leaned forward, her beautiful face alight with fascination. "You don't know that yet," she said. "The only thing we know for certain is that Pia is the *first* to see it."

"Fair enough," he growled. "But there are a lot of experienced magic users here, and several of them have been looking into the anomalies."

"That's true," the Elf murmured, her speculative gaze resting on Pia. Thoughtfully, she tapped one of her front teeth with a fingernail.

"And as it turns out, I happen to be a very experienced magic user, myself," Dragos pointed out. "I was in the same location as Pia, and I didn't see a damn thing."

Bel's gaze shifted from Pia to the dragon. "Not all magic is the same, as you know very well. I have no doubt that you are at the height of your Power, but you are not an Elf, and I cannot breathe fire. And neither one of us can call a thunderstorm like Tiago can. Pia may not be the only one who can see the creature. But that doesn't mean we will *all* be able to. Do you think this is connected to the sense you got of something being in your house?"

"Oh, boy." Pia thought back over the two events. "Yes, I believe so."

"Why do you think you saw it today and not yesterday?"

She lifted her shoulders in a shrug. "I reacted a lot quicker this morning. Maybe I looked in the right place at the right time? Maybe it helped that it was outside, and the sun was shining? It was a lot brighter than it was in our bedroom. All of this is speculation, of course. Your guess is as good as mine."

Tiago said, "There might not be only one of them. There could be more."

Graydon pinched his lower lip. His daughter rested on his lap, her tiny rosebud mouth open, occasionally making a slight squeak as she snored. "Why move things around and collapse the building site? Is it—or are they—trying to get our attention, or are they like cats and knocking shit over for the hell of it? If they want to get our attention, they've achieved that. But what are they trying to say?"

"That's assuming they're the ones that made the building collapse, and we don't know that either. Let's get back to trying to identify it," Dragos suggested. "That might give us some idea of its motive. What is it?"

Niniane lay on the floor, curled on her side as she played with Niall's plump fingers. She remarked wistfully, "It sounds like an angel." When everybody fell silent to stare at her, her expression turned self-conscious. "Or at least, it sounds like how I imagine an angel might look."

Bel's smile deepened. "In ancient Elven lore, there are creatures called the seraph that are not quite of this world. They are, we believe, the origin of the angelic beings described in Judaism, Christianity, and Islam. Personally, I've never seen one."

Dragos's eyes narrowed. "What do you mean, *not quite of this world?* I don't much care for the sound of anything that I can't see, hear, touch, taste, or kill."

Once Beluviel had hated and feared Dragos, as he and the Elves had a long, acrimonious history, but now she gave him a look filled with, Pia could have sworn, sincere affection. "Of course, you don't. The Great Beast is very much grounded in the material world."

Pia said suddenly, "Every Other land is in another dimension from Earth, and they're all connected with crossover passageways. What if these seraphs are in yet another dimension that comes very close to overlapping the ones we live in? We already know we live in a multiverse. Earth is not in the same place as Rhyacia, or Adriyel, or Ys. So by that logic, wouldn't it be possible for the seraph to exist on yet another neighboring plane?"

"You're making my head hurt," Niniane said cheerfully.

Dragos leaned back, stretched out his legs and crossed his arms and ankles. He stared at the ceiling.

"What I don't like about that idea is that it appears they can affect things on our plane, but that doesn't mean we can affect things on theirs." He said to Pia, "I'm not saying you're wrong. I'm saying I don't like it."

"Apparently, you don't like anything about the seraph," Bel murmured, sounding amused. He lifted his head to glare at the Elven woman.

"We don't even know yet if that's what it is," Pia said, suppressing a smile.

"According to our lore, the Elves were sometimes able to see and speak to the seraph," Bel said. "But we only just arrived in Rhyacia a few days before you did. Tomorrow, I would like to send some of my people out in teams to see what they can discover." She glanced at Graydon. "Maybe we can join them. If there are seraph here, I don't believe they would do anything to harm a child."

Dragos said, "We shouldn't relax any precautions until we know for certain one way or another."

"No, of course not."

While they talked, Dragos received a hand-delivered report that the construction crew at the concert hall had cleared the site and had begun digging below the foundation. They were using telekinesis to shift away soil and planned on working through the evening to take advantage of the cooler temperature, and the foreman would let Dragos know if they discovered anything.

The group lingered for a while longer but came to no further conclusions. Finally, Dragos and Pia gathered up

Niall and headed home to be greeted with extreme ecstasy by Skeeter.

"You have no dignity," Dragos told the dog.

Not only did Skeeter have no dignity, he clearly didn't care as he leaped and pranced about. Laughing, Pia went to the kitchen to discover what Jocasta and Ramone had made them for dinner. She discovered a large pork roast cooked to perfection for Dragos, along with fresh baked bread, and a salad for her made with grilled strips of jackfruit and avocadoes.

Mmm, grilled jackfruit. Her mouth watered. She was still wearing the leather pants and half armor, and she'd slung her bow and quiver of arrows on her back for the walk home, so she left Niall with his father and went to change.

Partway down the hall, the floor began to shake. Pia flung out a hand to brace herself against the wall. Skeeter howled.

"Dragos?" she called out.

"Don't panic," he called back. "It's an earthquake. Get outside."

The closest path to outside was through the master suite. Staggering through the bedroom, she stumbled onto the deck just as Dragos loped around the corner of the house, the baby on his shoulder. "Are you all right?"

"Yes." She looked around at the others in their little village exiting their houses. As Eva raced over, a deep rumbling rolled over them. Dread pulsed. "What is that?"

"People are telepathizing reports to me. Other construction sites are collapsing," Dragos said. He met her gaze. "Are you going to stay here with the baby?"

"What?" Waggling her head, she sassed, "Are *you* going to stay here with the baby?"

He pointed at her. "I had precedence for asking."

She knew he did, but she wasn't going to let him off the hook that easily. She made a face at him and turned to Eva.

Before she could say a word, Eva said, "Of course."

Eva took Niall from Dragos, who shapeshifted into the dragon. He bent his head so Pia could climb on, and once she was seated securely, he launched into the air.

He quickly climbed to a height that allowed them to see the full extent of the damage. They both fell silent as they took in the scene. *All* of the other construction sites had collapsed, and deep depressions indicated the presence of several sinkholes.

A dusty brown haze smeared the evening sky, and the largest sinkhole of all gaped at the concert hall site.

A flutter of movement caused Pia to look up.

Barely seen and transparent, dozens upon dozens of radiant creatures like the one she had seen earlier swooped and whirled in the evening sky overhead.

Chapter Eight

"OH, FUCK ME," the dragon muttered irascibly. "If it's not one damn thing, it's another."

He arrowed over to the concert hall construction site. As he landed, Pia jumped to the ground and he shapeshifted. Several workers ran over. One of them was the foreman.

"My lord!" he exclaimed. "We lost two men in the collapse. They fell into the sinkhole. We're searching for them now."

Dragos and Pia raced to peer down into the hole. It was even more massive close up, and deeper than Pia expected. The bottom was lost in shadow. A couple workers were climbing carefully down the rubble.

Power coalesced around Dragos. He extended one hand toward the hole, and a ball of light exploded from his fingertips. It fell like a meteor, and for a moment the darkness below was completely illuminated.

Pia glimpsed a segment of a large broken column, lying on its side, along with the base of other columns, and a rubble-strewn floor. "Those are ruins!"

"I see one of the men at the bottom. He's not

moving." Dragos looked at Pia. "We need to get down there."

"Ready when you are." If the man was still alive, she might be able to do something for him.

He scooped her up and the bottom fell out of her stomach as he leaped into the hole. As he landed, he absorbed the shock of impact by bending his legs, then he straightened and set her on her feet.

They picked their way over to the unmoving figure. The illumination from the sunlight above was indirect and slanted. Pia got the impression of a large space arching into darkness. Kneeling, she felt at the unconscious man's neck for a pulse.

"He's alive," she said with relief.

Dragos's Power flexed again as he scanned the man. "Couple broken ribs and a concussion."

I can help him, she said telepathically. All she had to do was prick her finger and let a little of her blood trickle into the unconscious man's mouth, and all his injuries would be healed. *We're far enough away from the surface, the others shouldn't sense anything.*

He shook his head. *He's not in danger of dying. Besides, if you heal him, by the time we get him to the surface he wouldn't have any injury at all, and that would cause speculation. It's not worth the risk of exposure.*

What he said made sense, but it was still difficult to hold back. Dragos cast a few simple healing spells while she assessed the area.

The other rescuers had located the second victim

partway down the hill of rubble, and they were in the process of lifting his limp figure out.

Watching the rescue from below, she decided jumping down into the hole for Dragos was a lot easier than trying to jump out. The cavernous space was big enough for him to change into his dragon form, but he wouldn't have enough room to launch out of the opening. The dragon could climb his way out, but with his massive size and weight she was pretty sure that would cause more collapse.

She shouted, "We need a stretcher down here!"

One of the people working at the surface shouted back in reply, "We've almost got one ready!"

They lowered a stretcher down. Dragos picked up the man and they strapped him in. Tugging on the rope, he stepped back, and they watched the rescuers haul him up.

"You guys okay down there?" a familiar voice called down. Graydon had arrived on the scene.

"Yes," Dragos shouted. "We're going to need ropes to get back out—but first, I want to have a look around." He looked at Pia. "Are you coming?"

What? Widening her eyes, she waggled her head, silently sassing him. Fill in the blank, Dragos.

He grinned. "I heard what you said, and you didn't utter a word. I don't know how you did that."

"You know me so well."

His amusement died as he turned his attention to the cavernous area. "What a clusterfuck."

"I know, but you had the area surveyed and assessed before anybody started building here. You did everything you could." She scratched along the edge of her jaw with one fingernail. "Who was it that recently mentioned something about ancient buried Roman cities?"

"I think this is much older than a Roman city. It takes thousands of years of sedimentation and soil erosion to bury something this deep, and I discovered this Other land only a few hundred years ago. Whoever once lived here was long gone by then." He held out his hand, igniting another ball of fire. His Power intensified as he held it up, and gradually the light grew to fill the space, illuminating what appeared to be a great hall. He took her hand. "There might be another collapse. Stay close."

They walked past giant shadowed columns covered in carvings. Dust lay thick on the floor, but in patches she could see a faint, complex mosaic, and murals carved in stone towered the height of three men.

"You don't have to worry. I have no intention of stepping out on my own." As they walked forward, she laced her fingers through his. "This may be splendid and fascinating, but it's also creepy."

"It *is* creepy," he agreed. "Ruins usually feel more peaceful."

She stared at one panel of a mural. It appeared to be the scene of a great battle. There was a huge army on the ground and winged creatures overhead. One figure on the ground appeared bigger than the others. He wore a crown that shone with a dim glint of gold and pointed a scepter or weapon toward the winged creatures in the sky.

That reminded her. "When we were on our way over here, I saw a lot more of the creatures flying overhead."

"Did you?" he said absently. He strode forward, pulling her along with him. "See that large rectangular stone on a dais? We seem to have a sarcophagus here. This entire hall may be a tomb."

Carvings covered the giant rectangle of stone, and more sparks of gold glinted in the reflection of Dragos's witchlight. A pile of rubble and large stones had damaged one end of the carved sarcophagus. A breath of wind blew against their faces with a dry rustle.

"The creatures seemed agitated." Her voice came out breathless. Was it her imagination or did the creepiness factor just kick up a notch or three? She stopped moving forward and tugged on Dragos's hand. "I don't want to go near the sarcophagus thingy."

The wind increased, bringing with it a darkness that enveloped them. Dragos's witchlight dimmed but did not quite go out, and his fingers crushed hers.

No really, he was crushing her hand. She felt caught in a vise of hot flame. "Dragos—you're hurting me!"

He turned to look at her. The expression on his face was indescribable. He whispered, "Run."

In agony now, she struggled to pull away from his grip. Then his hand loosened, his back arched, and he fell to the ground and convulsed. Oh shit oh shit *oh shit.*

Even as she dove to try to turn him onto his side, he exploded into his dragon form, the huge bronze body slapping into her. She tumbled backward and fell. With a sharp crack, the back of her head hit the floor.

Pain lanced through her skull. Dragos's witchlight had extinguished, and it was pitch black.

No, it was the faintest bit gray. Gradually her eyes adjusted. They had walked far enough from the sinkhole that very little light penetrated. The giant dragon lay immobile, and her soul echoed with emptiness.

The constant, often subtle presence of their mating bond had vanished.

"*Oh no no no no* NO NO NO...." Horror and wrongness yanked at her. Ignoring her body's flashes of pain, she sprang to her feet, cast her own witchlight and tossed it to the ground, and ran for the dragon's head. Her beautiful, strong, irascible mate *couldn't be dead. Not just like that.*

Stumbling over a rock, she fell onto the dragon's snout. Warmth curled from his nostril. He was breathing. She sobbed in relief, stroking his bronze hide. "Wake up!" she hissed at him. "You wake up."

Another breath of wind blew around her, carrying with it a hint of wings. Something did this to him. Something made him convulse. Leaping to her feet, she grabbed her bow, pulled an arrow, pointed it into the darkness. Her pulse thudded in her wrists and temples.

Dragos, she said telepathically. *I need you to wake up. You're the size of a six-seater Cessna. I can't move you on my own, and there's something down here in the dark with us. We'll figure out the mate thing later, just, wake up now, please. You have so much acreage I can't protect you if something attacks you on the other side. Please, please, baby. I need you to GET THE FUCK UP.*

The world flexed. The dragon shimmered and disappeared, and Dragos's human form lay sprawled on the ground. She backed over to him, knelt, and put her fingers to the carotid artery at his neck. That incredibly stubborn, ancient heart of his was still beating strong.

She still couldn't move him. As a human, he had to weigh close to three hundred pounds. Now what?

Just as she was about to scream as loud as she could for help from the surface, he opened his eyes and looked at her.

In the witchlight, his irises were amber.

Not gold.

He smiled. "Hello, darling. Aren't you a sight for sore eyes?"

Inside, she went cold and dark and numb.

Somehow, she made herself whisper, "You fell. Are you okay?"

"I believe so." He sat up and looked around. "We need to get out of here. I can't wait to be out in the open air again."

She made herself nod. "Let's go."

He rose to his feet and looked at the bow and arrow she still held in one hand. "There's no need for those weapons. All is well now. Put those away."

There was an incalculable amount of Power in his voice, held in check with a sure, steady control, like a hand on the reins of a dangerous stallion.

"All right." Her hands shook as she obeyed.

They walked back to the hole. The silence that fell around them was complete. No wings, no whispers, no dark wind. When they stepped into sight, Tiago had joined Graydon at the rim, and a rope dangled, waiting for them.

"After you, my beauty." He helped to adjust the loop of the rope underneath her foot, fingers lingering to caress her ankle. Her skin crawled. Somehow, she managed to keep from yanking away from him.

Graydon hauled her up easily, while Tiago and several others dropped another rope into the hole. She did a lot of thinking on that road to sunlight and fresh air, some of the fastest and most terrified thinking in her life. As soon as her feet connected to solid ground, she lunged at Graydon and grabbed his hands.

"What is it, cupcake?" he asked kindly. "You look like you've seen a ghost."

She very much feared that she had.

Gray, she said telepathically. *Don't speak out loud. Don't show any reaction.*

His gray gaze turned sharp. *Pia, what's wrong?*

The creature they're pulling out of the hole isn't Dragos.

He went still. *What do you mean?*

I didn't stutter. She dug her nails into his skin. *I went down into that hellhole with my mate, but he isn't coming back out with me. Do what I tell you to do and do it fast and quietly. Get Eva to take Niall away. I don't care where. Send Giselle with him, along with all the other children.*

Absolutely.

Who's the fastest winged Wyr here—you or Tiago?

Tiago, he said without hesitation.

Send him back to Earth. Tell him.... Out of the corner of her eye, she saw the man who looked like Dragos emerge from the hole. He grinned and clapped one of the rescuers on the shoulder, took a deep breath and squinted at the setting sun. Squinted. At the sun. A deep vibration started inside, like her bones were screaming. *Tell him to bring back every sentinel he can as quickly as possible. Tell him to get Liam. And tell him to say to Aryal that she once swore she would destroy the shackles that Niniane's uncle Urien made to imprison Dragos. Tiago will remember those all too well—that Dark Fae woman, whatever her name was, nearly destroyed him with those shackles. And Aryal promised to drop them in a volcano. Do you remember?*

Hell, of course I do. We all do.

Aryal never does anything she's supposed to. Pia's lips felt numb. *I hope to all the gods she didn't do what she was supposed to do then, either. We need those shackles, Gray—as quick as a Djinn can get them here. I will pay a Djinn any favor they like. You tell Tiago that.*

Graydon's rough-hewn features turned deadly. *I'm on it.*

Another thrill of terror froze her muscles. *Wipe that look off your face, damn it. Dragos is one of the oldest and most*

Powerful of the Elder Races—and that thing inhabiting his body took him down. So you smile like your life depends on it.

Even as she spoke, his expression eased into good-natured friendliness. Squeezing her fingers, he turned back to where Dragos appeared to be talking to the others. Graydon said, "Hell of a mess we've got here."

The imposter turned to him and smiled. "Indeed, it is. I look forward to reshaping our future. But for the moment, I decree that everyone stay well away from these holes. The collapsed soil is too dangerous, and there is nothing below we need concern ourselves with for now." He told the foreman, "Set a barrier here with guards."

Beside him, Tiago frowned, and his eyes grew sharp, but no one else appeared to notice anything amiss. She wanted to scream at them. *Dragos doesn't talk that way!*

Instead, she smiled at the imposter. "It's been a difficult day. I suggest we throw off these setbacks and convene on the beach for a feast, and people can bring whatever they have to share."

The imposter gestured and raised his voice. "My lady has an excellent idea! What say you to a feast?"

Several cheers went up. Smiling, the imposter strolled to Pia and gazed into her eyes. Fingering the ends of her hair, he murmured, "We will have wine and sweetmeats, and celebrate life, and later on I would celebrate alone with my wife in our bed."

Out of the corner of her eye, she saw Graydon stiffen, and—God love him, he was no actor—he turned homicidal. Sharply, she said in his head, *Do your job. I've got this.*

Gray growled to Tiago, "I need a word with you. Now."

Meanwhile, Pia drew her fingers across the imposter's lips. "It will be my pleasure to celebrate in any way my lord sees fit."

Chapter Nine

N EARLY TWENTY THOUSAND people gathered along the shore of the lake to party. Musicians brought their instruments, and bonfires were built. There was dancing, and all manner of food was hastily assembled. The Demonkind brought barrels of liquor. And if there were no children present, and if one or two people looked at the imposter with troubled, cold expressions, nobody remarked upon it.

Pia excused herself to put on makeup and dress in a skirt and halter top. She pinned up her hair and let loose tendrils fall down on her neck, and she painted her lips with her favorite lipstick. Skeeter was restless while she prepared, whining and growling at turns while he paced. Afraid that the imposter might harm him, she made Jocasta and Ramone take him away.

And she flirted with that bastard with everything she had. She fed him bites of pastries, and grilled meats, and kissed him in between drinks of wine, and let him fondle her breast. She had never fought a war like this before, but she threw everything she had into it.

He laughed often, that thief of everything. Amber

eyes flashing, he spoke with many, and his restless gaze roamed over the females in the crowd with speculative intent, but his gaze always came back to Pia.

How long would it take for Tiago to fly to the nearest crossover passageway? She knew the approximate answer to that one: it took Dragos a couple of hours to fly here. But Dragos had been moving at a leisurely pace. Tiago would be flying with all the strength and speed he could muster.

Then it would take him a few minutes to confer with Malan, and another five to ten minutes to cross the passageway back to Earth. He could call New York from the Earth-side guard station. And she knew from experience the sentinels always kept go-bags packed and could mobilize in an instant.

But she didn't know how long it would take Aryal to retrieve the shackles from wherever she might have hidden them—if she had in fact hidden them and not destroyed them, as she had promised. And Pia had no idea how long it might take them to negotiate for a quick passage back with a Djinn.

Each beat of her heart felt as long as a year, and the burden of continuing without the support of feeling the mating bond weighed heavily. That was the thing about fighting a war—you never knew if you would live or die.

It helped that she wasn't alone. Beluviel had not left with the children. Instead, the Elven woman watched the imposter with an assessing gaze from the other side of a bonfire, and every one of her attendants was armed.

Graydon interrupted the imposter often to pull him aside and ask him this or that, and at one point, Linwe sauntered over to invite the imposter to dance. He went with a flare of illicit interest. Pia turned away, pretending not to notice.

She was also attended by a tall, slender-winged creature on either side. No one else except perhaps the Elves saw them, but as the interminable evening wore on, they gradually became more visible to her. They looked at her with what appeared to be compassion in their radiant eyes, but when they turned to the imposter their inhuman faces grew sharp as swords.

When Pia finally saw Rune and Carling walk arm-and-arm through the crowd, just like two more partygoers, she nearly lost it. Liam strolled past, his powerful body moving with the same liquid, dangerous grace as his father. He glanced at her once, blue gaze and handsome features inscrutable.

Then there was Bayne, and Aryal and Quentin, Grym, Tiago and Graydon, each one moving as if by random and disconnected from the others. All the sentinels had arrived except for Alexander, who must be the sentinel left in charge in New York. She even saw the Djinn Khalil and Grace, the Oracle, who stared at the unseen in wonder.

Pia walked away midsentence from the Vampyre she'd been talking with. She approached the imposter who was deep in conversation with a laughing sylphlike Wyr woman who was clueless about what was really going on and thought she was flirting with Pia's husband and mate.

Pia tucked her arm into the imposter's and said to the woman, "I'll remember you, you little shit."

That wiped away the other woman's smile. Gulping, she slipped away. The imposter turned to Pia with a twinkle. Apparently, he enjoyed acrimony. "That was rather unsporting of you, my darling."

"I'm tired of fucking around," she told him. "Are you going to dance with me or not?"

He gave her a mocking bow. "I am yours to command, lady wife."

She led him to one side and pulled his hands onto her hips. Dragos's hands. They felt so familiar she wanted to scream in rage and pain.

As he smilingly drew her closer, Rune walked up behind him and wound the chain from one of the shackles around his neck. Astonished fury exploded across his face. When he erupted into violence, Liam slammed into him, pinning his arms to his side. The other sentinels, both former and present, leaped into the fray. Graydon lunged past Pia, shoving her back from the fight so hard she fell and rolled away.

Shouts and screams, and a general scramble ensued. Bel and her attendants raced to surround Pia. Grace, Niniane, and Khalil herded people back from the fight.

Pia ignored it all as she brushed off sand and stood. Her entire attention was focused on the writhing pile of warriors.

All the sentinels were deadly, but Dragos was the fastest and deadliest of all. The only one who was truly his match in strength and speed was Liam. And she prayed with everything she had that the imposter could not fully access all of Dragos's abilities, and he did not fully understand the true nature of the body he had stolen.

Vicious though it was, the battle was over in short order. Confined by the magic in the shackles, the imposter was overwhelmed by the sheer strength in the numbers allied against him. One by one they lifted away, until he lay on the sand, bound by magicked metal, his face distorted with towering rage.

Carling had joined Pia to watch the battle, her beautiful features intent. The ancient Vampyre was one of the most experienced and deadly magic users Pia had ever met. If anyone might know how to exorcise the creature who had taken over Dragos's body, it was her.

Pia whispered, "How do we expel it?"

Carling's large, almond shaped eyes were compassionate. "I don't know, Pia. I had hoped the null spell shackles would force it out, but it appears that it hasn't."

"There has to be something we can do. Anything." As Grace, the young woman who was the Oracle, limped up to them, Pia whirled to her. "Grace? Did you see something useful?"

Grace shook her head, mouth downturned. "There were too many people milling about, and now that he's bound, the shackles are preventing me from seeing anything. I'm so sorry. I wish I had something useful to offer."

Panic started shrieking in her head. Ruthlessly, she squashed it. Panic wasn't going to get Dragos back. She walked over to the sprawled figure and knelt beside him. "Give me back my husband."

"Your husband is dead," the imposter spat. His nose had been bloodied and droplets sprayed her face.

She didn't flinch. Instead she leaned closer and stared into his eyes. "If my husband is dead," she said, "then I have nothing to lose, do I?"

He started to laugh then convulsed. Briefly—oh so briefly—hot gold flashed in his eyes. Dragos snarled telepathically, *Do what you need to do.*

The next minute, Dragos was gone again, and the creature who glared back at her had eyes of amber. It hurt so bad to see him so briefly, yet at the same time triumph swelled. Somehow, somewhere, her mate was still in there.

And she would do whatever she needed to get him back.

"This is going to suck really badly for you," she told the imposter. "Because my husband's body is incredibly strong, and he can survive a lot of abuse." Standing, she avoided looking at Liam. She said to the sentinels who ringed them, "Question him. Do whatever it takes."

Then she walked away. They moved to close the gap behind her, and Dragos disappeared from view.

To be continued in The Adversary

Thank you!

Dear Readers,

Thank you for reading *The Unseen*! I hope you enjoyed returning to Dragos and Pia as much as I enjoyed writing them. They have been two of my favorite characters of all time, and they'll always occupy a special place in my heart.

The Unseen is the first of two linked stories with all new Dragos and Pia adventures. They want to be told in a different way than I have written previous stories in the Elder Races, so please be warned: there is a cliffhanger at the end of the first novella. Everything will be resolved in the second book, and it will not end in a cliffhanger.

Would you like to stay in touch and hear about new releases? You can:

- Sign up for my monthly email at www.theaharrison.com
- Follow me on Twitter at @TheaHarrison
- Like my Facebook page at facebook.com/TheaHarrison

Reviews help other readers find the books they like to read. I appreciate each and every review, whether positive or negative.

Happy reading! – And keep scrolling for a sneak peek at the cover art for *The Adversary*!

~Thea

Look for these titles from Thea Harrison

THE ELDER RACES SERIES – FULL LENGTH NOVELS

Published by Berkley

Dragon Bound

Storm's Heart

Serpent's Kiss

Oracle's Moon

Lord's Fall

Kinked

Night's Honor

Midnight's Kiss

Shadow's End

MOONSHADOW TRILOGY

Moonshadow

Spellbinder

Lionheart

AMERICAN WITCH TRILOGY

American Witch

THE CHRONICLES OF RHYACIA

The Unseen

The Adversary

ELDER RACES NOVELLAS

True Colors

Natural Evil

Devil's Gate

Hunter's Season

The Wicked

Dragos Takes a Holiday

Pia Saves the Day

Peanut Goes to School

Dragos Goes to Washington

Pia Does Hollywood

Liam Takes Manhattan

The Chosen

Planet Dragos

ELDER RACES SERIES COLLECTIONS

Divine Tarot

Destiny's Tarot

The Elder Races Tarot Collection: All 4 Stories

A Dragon's Family Album

A Dragon's Family Album II

A Dragon's Family Album: Final Collection

The Elder Races: Complete Novella Bundle 2013-2018

GAME OF SHADOWS SERIES
Published by Berkley

Rising Darkness
Falling Light

ROMANCES UNDER THE NAME
AMANDA CARPENTER

E-published by Samhain Publishing
(original publication by Harlequin Mills & Boon)
These stories are currently out of print

A Deeper Dimension
The Wall
A Damaged Trust
The Great Escape
Flashback
Rage
Waking Up
Rose-Coloured Love
Reckless
The Gift of Happiness
Caprice
Passage of the Night
Cry Wolf
A Solitary Heart
The Winter King